PUFFIN BOOKS

NOWHERE

Jon Robinson was born in Middlesex in 1983. When he's not writing, he works for a charity in central London. *Nowhere* is his first published novel. Find out more about Jon at:

www.facebook.com/jonrobinsonbooks

NOWHERE

JON ROBINSON

PUFFIN

PUFFIN BOOKS

Published by the Penguin Group
Penguin Books Ltd, 80 Strand, London WC2R ORL, England
Penguin Group (USA) Inc., 375 Hudson Street, New York, New York 10014, USA
Penguin Group (Canada), 90 Eglinton Avenue East, Suite 700, Toronto, Ontario, Canada M4P 2Y3
(a division of Pearson Penguin Canada Inc.)
Penguin Ireland, 25 St Stephen's Green, Dublin 2, Ireland (a division of Penguin Books Ltd)
Penguin Group (Australia), 707 Collins Street, Melbourne, Victoria 3008, Australia
(a division of Pearson Australia Group Pty Ltd)
Penguin Books India Pvt Ltd, 11 Community Centre, Panchsheel Park,
New Delhi – 110 017, India
Penguin Group (NZ), 67 Apollo Drive, Rosedale, Auckland 0632, New Zealand
(a division of Pearson New Zealand Ltd)
Penguin Books (South Africa) (Pty) Ltd, Block D, Rosebank Office Park,
181 Jan Smuts Avenue, Parktown North, Gauteng 2193, South Africa

Penguin Books Ltd, Registered Offices: 80 Strand, London WC2R ORL, England

puffinbooks.com

First published 2013
001

Text copyright © Jon Robinson, 2013
All rights reserved

The moral right of the author has been asserted

Set in 11/15.5pt Sabon LT Std
Typeset by Jouve (UK), Milton Keynes
Printed in Great Britain by Clays Ltd, St Ives plc

British Library Cataloguing in Publication Data
A CIP catalogue record for this book is available from the British Library

ISBN: 978-0-141-34654-0

www.greenpenguin.co.uk

MIX
Paper from
responsible sources
FSC® C018179

Penguin Books is committed to a sustainable
future for our business, our readers and our planet.
This book is made from Forest Stewardship
Council™ certified paper.

ALWAYS LEARNING   **PEARSON**

To Mum and Sarah

1

Alyn came to with a start, coughing up clumps of snow. He lay dazed for some moments, watching his breath swirl: a silver plume, crumbling in the icy air.

'There he is,' said a voice, buried amid the roaring winds. 'He's down. Good shot.' The sound caused a crow to take flight from a nearby tree, releasing a cascade of tumbling snowflakes.

I didn't make it, Alyn thought. *After everything, I didn't escape* . . .

He felt winded and deflated, but somehow found the strength to struggle to his feet. At the far end of the yard, a line of wardens, clad in their black militaristic uniforms, were stomping towards him. Panic helped Alyn gather his bearings. He turned to the wire-mesh fence and sprinted towards it on stumbling legs.

'He's getting away,' came a cry. 'Get after him!'

Alyn threw himself at the fence, grabbing frantically at the wire with trembling fingers. *Climb*, he commanded, pulling himself up. *You can make it; there's not far to go.*

The nearest guard raised his ibis and fired. The shot hit the ground behind Alyn, sending up a spray of snow.

How – or why – his captors had access to such weaponry remained a mystery. The ibis resembled a simple baton, but was able to release a devastating blast of compressed sound. Unlike a gun or rifle, the ibis left no mark and spilled no blood, but this made the weapon no less dangerous, only whoever was using it even more so. Alyn suspected that had the guards ever been on the receiving end they might have been a little less keen to fire so willingly.

'Prisoner Hart!' shouted one of the approaching guards. 'Remove yourself from the fence immediately.'

Alyn peered over his shoulder at the five figures, then back up at the top of the fence. If he could make it to the woods, he might be able to lose them. There was a chance he might die of cold, but that would be better than returning to his cell. Anything would.

He dragged himself further up the fence, unable to feel his fingers.

Breath spilled from his mouth as he struggled with the wire. His lungs burned and his throat felt coarse and cut.

Another shot whizzed past him, wobbling the fence. He could hear the guards continue to advance, crunching through mounds of snow.

'Remove yourself from the fence,' the guard repeated, closer now. 'This is your final warning.'

I'm almost over, he told himself. *One last pull and I'm there . . . I'm free –*

Just as he was reaching for the top of the fence, the blast hit him between the shoulder-blades. Alyn opened his mouth, but only a croak left his lips. His fingers released and then he was falling, the fence retreating from him.

The last thing that flashed through his mind was not so much a thought but a picture. A phantom image of how things might have been: of him sprinting away through the trees to freedom. But now, like everything else, it was gone.

2

Jes was vacantly watching the falling snow through the steamed canteen windows at the rear of the prison. The room was narrow and low-ceilinged, barely containing the horde of a hundred or so grey uniforms.

Jes combed her fingers through her straight red hair. At any moment the bell would sound and those who had afternoon chores, herself included, would be gathered up and herded outside into the cold.

A ripple of mutters and murmurs swept through the room as the guards emerged through the double doors, dragging an unconscious Alyn behind them. Jes sprang up from her chair and sped through the rows of tables towards the door.

'What have you done to him?' she said, trying to manoeuvre round the procession of guards.

'Get back,' said the nearest warden.

'But I need to –'

The man pointed the ibis at her chest. 'I said *get back*.'

Jes froze. She could see from the look in his eyes that she was on the verge of going too far. 'Alyn!' she called across, not advancing a step further. 'Can you hear me? What happened? What did they –'

'Put him there,' announced the chief warden, Martin Adler, nodding his shaven head towards the nearest table. 'I want them all to see him.'

The men carrying Alyn tossed him on to a busy table, knocking a couple of plastic cups and a cold bowl of soup to the floor. The inmates quickly dispersed. Alyn lay still, except for the shallow rise and fall of his chest.

'We caught him trying to escape,' Adler announced, silencing the nervous chatter in the canteen. He walked slowly round the table, circling the unconscious boy. 'After all this time there are *still* those of you who don't want to accept your guilt! Those of you who don't want to be rehabilitated. To change. To grow. We've given you too many chances. And this –' Adler pointed at Alyn with his ibis – 'is the last. The next one of you to screw up means *all* of you will face the consequences. So, if any of your peers get any ideas about leaving, I suggest you try to persuade them otherwise. Is that understood?'

The room answered quietly but affirmatively in unison, eyes downcast.

Adler pushed past the other guards to leave the room. 'You won't ever escape!' he shouted without looking back, spit flying from his mouth. 'There's nothing out there for you. Not any more.'

Jes bit down on her lip, trying to suppress the anger that had gathered in knots in the pit of her stomach.

Alyn's skin seemed even more sallow than usual and his jagged black fringe hung over his eyes. Jes watched helplessly as the guards dragged him through the double doors to the cells.

Julian, a slim sixteen-year-old, had quietly slithered up beside her. 'I'm sure he'll be all right,' he said, his pointed features struggling to suppress a smirk.

Jes shot him such a fierce look that her green eyes seemed almost as red as her hair.

'They weren't lying,' he went on. 'I saw everything. He was a fool.'

'He was brave. Something you'd know nothing about.'

'A brave man is just a fool who gets lucky.' Julian started to walk away, but then turned back to her and added, 'I guess Alyn didn't.'

The familiar sight of the barred door came sliding into focus as Alyn awoke. The cell was a drab, rectangular alcove, with two beds beneath the reinforced window. Bars on one side divided the neighbouring cell, whilst the other was hidden from view by a brick wall.

With some considerable effort, Alyn pulled himself up to a sitting position on the thin mattress and gazed at the unforgiving landscape. It seemed like it had been winter forever.

The prison, at least what he knew of it, was little more than a concrete cube surrounded by acres of woodland. Only two rows of windows broke the brutal monotony of its stained, weather-beaten exterior. A wire fence encircled the compound, with a set of gates and an imposing solitary lookout tower at the front, and an allocated exercise yard at the back. The fence extended deep underground – so much so that crawling beneath it was out of the question. The front and sides were off-limits to the inmates.

Alyn pressed his face to the window, and his breath steamed the reinforced glass. Inside, things were just as hopeless. The cells took up half of the building: two tiers in a breezeblock hall, with a walkway running along the upper level, and wardens standing sentry in the centre. While he was lost in thought, a couple of guards appeared at the foot of his cell with a curly-haired boy not much older than sixteen.

'You may as well make yourself at home,' the tallest guard said, yanking open the barred door and shoving him towards the empty bed across from Alyn's. 'You're going to be here for a while.'

As soon as the door closed, Alyn's new cellmate sprang back towards it and started pulling and pounding at the bars.

'I've not done anything wrong!' he yelled. '*I'm*

innocent! Do you hear me? I've not done anything –
let me out!'

Alyn watched him scream and shout until his
northern accent grew hoarse.

'They aren't listening. I've been here long enough
to know that.'

The boy spun round, until then unaware that he
wasn't alone.

'Who are you?'

'Your cellmate by the look of things. I'm Alyn.'

He extended his hand. The boy looked at it, then
up at Alyn and turned back to the door.

'Ryan.' The boy threw his name over his shoulder.

Alyn lowered his hand and winced as a pulse of
white-hot pain flared between his shoulder-blades.

'Hang on,' the boy said, examining his cellmate's
grey boiler suit. 'Why are you here?'

'Same reason you are. *I'm a criminal.*'

'A criminal?'

'There are a hundred of us here,' Alyn told him.
'Boys and girls, between thirteen and eighteen, from
all over the country. We're all criminals . . .'

'But?'

'But none of us remember committing any crimes.'

'I know *I* haven't done anything,' Ryan said,
lowering his voice. 'We can't all be wrong, can we?'

'It's us versus them,' Alyn said. 'We tell them we're

innocent; they tell us we're guilty. On and on, back and forth like a game. So far, they're winning.'

'How?'

'Because some of us have even started to believe it. See that girl over there?'

Ryan looked over at a blonde girl in a cell on the far side of the hall, sitting on her bed with her arms round her legs.

'She was brought in about a year ago, not long after me. Apparently, they abducted her one night after school and next thing she's in that cell. They told her she tried robbing a jeweller's. Held a knife to the owner's throat. Of course, she denied it at first . . .'

'And?'

Disappointment showed on Alyn's face. 'Then she started questioning herself – maybe she *had* done it. Maybe she had amnesia, or something. Maybe she was going crazy. After all, they don't just arrest people for no reason, do they? She started off doubting them, then herself, and now . . .'

'Now what?'

'Now she'll tell you everything from the kind of necklace she stole to the shirt the owner was wearing.'

It took several moments for this to sink in. 'You're telling me she was brainwashed or something?'

'We prefer to call it *turned*. They can be very persuasive.'

Ryan gave an uncomfortable laugh. 'This is crazy. You're crazy.'

Alyn said nothing and watched him pace back and forth between the window and the door. He eventually came to a halt.

'They haven't *turned* you yet, have they?'

'Not yet.'

'They won't get me. There's no way.' Ryan dragged his fingers through his dirty-blond hair. 'I won't let them.'

'They'll start by getting you to sign a confession. They'll have your papers ready by this evening.'

'I'm not signing anything.' The boy mumbled something else under his breath and resumed pounding the bars again. When he reluctantly ceased some minutes later, the skin on his hands was flayed and split and speckled with blood.

Alyn watched him. 'I would've told you to stop. But maybe it's healthy to be angry. You'll be confused next, then compliant. Then all you'll think about is escape. It'll be the first thing you think of in the morning and the last thing at night. Then when you can't even think about escape any more, you'll just . . .' Alyn trailed off, then added regretfully, 'You won't even think about anything.'

The boy massaged his sore hands and, letting out a heavy sigh, he said, 'Sounds like you've been here too long.'

Alyn wasn't going to argue.

Ryan studied Alyn for a few lingering seconds then walked to the window.

'So where the hell are we?'

'*Nowhere.*'

'Am I gonna get a straight answer out of you or –'

'That's what they call it. *Nowhere.* And, before you ask, they made sure we were unconscious when they brought us, so it's not like we even know how far away we are from anything.'

'What kind of prison won't even tell the prisoners where they are?'

'One like this.'

Ryan wiped the fog on the chilled glass with his sleeve and peered out, cupping his eyes from the reflection.

'What else do you know about *Nowhere*?'

'It's one of the few words in the dictionary that doesn't have a synonym,' Alyn quipped.

'You don't say. What about those stick things the guards carry? I've never seen anything like them before. It's like they're magic wands or something. Or from the future . . .'

'*Ibises.* The guards treat them like they're toys. I once saw them shoot a kid who was taking too long to finish his dinner. They hurt. And if you get shot here with one –' Alyn tapped the side of his head – 'chances are you'll forget the last couple of hours. I thought I was going mad at first.'

'Explains why my memory's a little cloudy. I wonder where they got them from.'

'I used to have a friend who was convinced that the most powerful people in the world have access to technology a hundred years more advanced than anything the rest of us know about. I always said he was crazy. Now I'm starting to think he might have had a point.'

'What makes you think that the most powerful people in the world are involved in this?'

'Take a look around,' Alyn said. 'What makes you think they *aren't*?'

Ryan held Alyn's eyes for a couple of moments then deflected the comment with a shrug. 'So why don't you tell me what your crime is?' he said.

'Arson. They say I set fire to a house. There was someone living in it, an old tramp . . .'

'They're saying you killed someone?'

'Accidentally. But yeah. That's what they're saying.'

'And you don't remember a thing? There must be someone who knows where we are . . . What about my parents, my friends? They're just going to think I disappeared –'

'I guess that's kind of the point.'

But, before Alyn could say another word, a group of figures convened outside the cell and in stepped a woman in her forties, dark hair pulled back in a bun, wearing a blazer and knee-length skirt. Her expression was stern, as though it had been sculpted by years of contempt.

'Ryan Farrell?'

'Who are you?'

'I suppose you could think of me as a kind of *teacher*. You're coming with me to the interrogation room. We'll be having a little chat.'

'About time. This is a big mistake.'

'You've got a lot to learn, Farrell, starting with knowing when to shut up. Now let's walk.'

'Bye,' Alyn said. 'See you again soon.'

'Not if I can help it.'

You can't, Alyn thought, and he watched the group forcefully lead Ryan out of the cell and turn left on to the walkway.

3

'Heads. *Again,*' Harlan said, and closed his fist round the silver coin.

Harlan was a tall, dark-skinned boy with black hair, who had only recently turned seventeen. At least, he thought he had. There were no calendars or clocks in the prison: nothing to keep track of the endless free fall of days and nights. As if to heighten the disorientation, even the routines varied between inmates, with some being sent to work while others slept.

'What are you talking about now, Harlan?' said the boy in the cell beside his, peering at him through the bars.

'The coin. It landed on heads twenty-three times in a row. It's not weighted on one side,' Harlan said. 'There's no reason why it should . . .'

'There's no reason it shouldn't. Didn't you do probability in school? If you flip a coin enough times, you start seeing patterns.'

Harlan opened his hand and inspected the coin. He turned it in his palm until it glinted in the weak light.

'You think it's meaningless.'

'When you spend all day flipping a coin and noticing how it lands, it *means* you've been here way too long. And there's only one thing that will get you out of here. *Confess*.'

Harlan didn't look up. 'I have confessed. Every day I've confessed. Over and over . . .'

'You say it but you don't mean it.'

'You've confessed,' Harlan said. 'So why are you still here? Why has no one left?'

After some moments' thought, the boy shrugged. 'They have their reasons. Perhaps we still need to learn.' He slunk away from the bars and lay tiredly on his mattress.

Harlan rolled the coin between his knuckles like a casino chip and glanced at the wall on the other side of the cell. Although he figured it was probably nothing more than an architectural support, closer examination suggested it was hollow and wide enough for a person to fit inside. Where it led, if anywhere, was another question entirely.

He waited until his neighbour was asleep and tied a sheet over the exposed bars between the cells, as was often the case when they were getting dressed.

He reckoned there was a half-hour window before

any guards returned from overseeing the yard chores. Making sure no one was watching, Harlan slid beneath the bed and wriggled until he was level with the brick, then began carefully, quietly scratching at the cement with the coin.

'Now, let's not waste any time, Farrell.' The teacher opened the leather-bound folder she was carrying, and pushed open the door to the interrogation room, letting Ryan in, followed by a couple of guards. 'We both know why you're here –'

'Actually, no,' Ryan cut in. 'I don't. And it seems I'm not the only one. Is this a joke?'

'No.'

'A conspiracy then? It has to be. Who'd have the money and power to pull off something like this?'

'Conspiracy? I hope you're not implying we just drive around and arrest people for no good reason.' She accepted a coffee mug from the nearest guard.

'Yeah. That's how it looks.'

The teacher seemed amused. She walked behind a desk in the centre of the room and gestured for the guard beside Ryan to pull out a chair for him. Ryan looked at the chair suspiciously and finally sat.

'Do you have any idea how much it costs to house a prisoner per year? And teenagers – a hundred of you under the same roof? *Willingly?* You must think we're mad . . .'

'Pretty much. Now, are you going to tell me where I am, or –'

'That's confidential.'

'Why – because we're so dangerous? Or because you don't want anybody to find us?'

'Have you been in trouble with the law before, Ryan?'

Ryan shifted uncomfortably.

'Vandalism, under-age drinking … *fighting*.' She turned the next page. 'It says here you've been expelled from two schools. Quite an achievement.'

'Last I heard, a bit of graffiti and a few playground scraps didn't get you put in Alcatraz.'

'This is a new initiative. We're cracking down harder on young offenders. Keeping the streets safe from the likes of you.'

'Keep telling yourself that. Some day you might believe it.'

'If you have another explanation I'd be delighted to hear it.'

'It's a lie, isn't it? All of it: the prison, the guards, everything. None of it's real.'

'Including me, Farrell?'

Ryan narrowed his eyes. 'Especially you.'

The teacher seemed genuinely concerned at hearing this. 'Have you had this sense of *unreality* before?'

'Never.'

'Well, I suppose sudden onsets do tend to be the

worst,' she said, her pen striking a mark on the page. 'You haven't experienced any kind of injuries since the crime, have you? Haven't had any blackouts or . . .'

'No, I haven't, because *there was no crime*!' He was unable to stop his voice from rising. 'There was no crime. I'm innocent, just like Alyn, just like everyone else here –'

'Alyn Hart is *not* innocent. He has a history of dangerous and reckless behaviour: drinking, drugs, violent outbursts. Even this morning he tried to escape and had to be restrained by several officers. Does that sound like the behaviour of an innocent young man to you, Ryan?'

'What do you expect him to do – just sit here and take it?'

'That's precisely how rehabilitation works, Ryan. You sit there and you take responsibility for what you've done, and for how you can go about changing. It's often a long and challenging process.'

She pushed the leather-bound folder to one side.

'What's in there?'

The teacher snatched the folder away before Ryan could take it. 'That's not for you, Farrell.'

Ryan sat back and folded his arms wearily. 'When are the lies going to end?'

'Opposition to authority,' she noted. 'Have you always had such a negative attitude towards your superiors?'

She's delusional. They all are.

'We know from your files that you're short-tempered, aggressive. Prone to lashing out. Do you have any remorse?'

Ryan's heart was slamming against his chest. He felt flushed and faint. 'For the last time, I didn't ... do ... *anything*. I'm not guilty!'

'Would you like me to explain to you what you did?' The teacher waited for a response, which never came, and said, 'You stole some alcohol from the off-licence near your home on the night of the twenty-eighth of November. You got drunk. You then stole your friend's father's car and you sped along the high street, endangering the lives of countless other motorists, before being involved in a head-on collision with a second car. You escaped unscathed, Ryan. But the driver of the second car, a twenty-three-year-old art student, didn't. She passed away before she even reached the hospital.'

Ryan felt the colour draining from his face. *Why were they doing this? It was such an elaborate game ...*

'Do you remember now? Do you have any remorse for what you did? For that poor girl's life you took with your ... stupidity?'

Ryan opened his mouth to speak but no sound came out.

'I'll take that as a no. No remorse for crime.'

Dizzy with frustration, Ryan sprang out of his

chair and threw a frantic, desperate punch at the nearest guard. The impact was enough to send the man reeling back. He reached out, trying to stop his fall, and knocked the coffee mug to the floor.

Before Ryan could move away, he was grabbed by the other guard. He gritted his teeth and, turning, leapt forward in a headbutt. He felt the man's nose give against his forehead.

The teacher snatched the radio from the fallen man's belt. 'Send back-up,' she shouted. 'Now!'

Ryan sped out of the room and along the corridor, trying to remember which way they had taken him. An ibis blast whizzed by, close enough to tingle the hairs on his arm.

Ryan quickly descended the stairs at the end of the corridor, emerging into the front hall. Stirred by the sound of the commotion, many of the prisoners had already appeared at the bars of their cells in anticipation. He whirled back and forth, unable to focus on the panorama of surrounding faces.

A set of double doors opened and three guards spilled out, weapons raised.

Ryan halted. He turned round to find a second group of guards blocking his exit. He presented his fists, unable to disguise his trembling hands.

'You're in a lot of trouble,' said Claude Rayner, Adler's deputy. Rayner stepped through the crowd of men.

'Teach him a lesson, Claude,' one of the other guards said, then almost wilted as Rayner glared at him.

Ryan looked at Rayner's weapon, then into his cold grey eyes. There was the soft whistle of parting air from the ibis barrel, and then nothing.

4

Two years ago

Just as the Prime Minister was leaving the stage that evening, a sudden rain began to fall. He hurried down the steps, flanked by two aides.

'That didn't go down well,' he murmured as rain pinged the umbrella fabric. 'Let's get out of here.'

Once they had escaped the eager reporters, the jousting microphones and clattering camera shutters, the Prime Minister turned down a cordoned-off alleyway in the shadows.

'Sir,' said one of his aides. 'Isn't the car supposed to be picking you up from over there?'

'Change of plan,' the Prime Minister said. 'I'll be going with someone else instead.'

He parted from them with a wave and pulled his coat tightly round him, hurrying through the rain.

The car was already waiting for him at the end of

the alleyway. He jogged towards it and tapped on the tinted window with his knuckles.

'I'm sorry. Things took a little longer than expected,' he said as the door opened.

'The important thing is that you're here,' said James Felix. Felix was a white-haired man of around sixty, dressed in an expensive tailored suit. His heavy-lidded eyes watched, sombrely.

The Prime Minister quickly climbed in beside him, beating the damp out of his coat. 'Let's get to the point, shall we? Why did you want to see me?' he said as the car set off.

Felix paused. His eyes flickered back and forth as though searching for the words. 'It appears that we might be in some sort of trouble. The country, I mean.'

The Prime Minister raised an eyebrow, peering through the wriggling raindrops on the window. 'This has come as a surprise? Unemployment and debt are at an all-time high. Crime is soaring. The unrest – and that is quite an understatement – is palpable.' He looked at Felix. 'We'll be lucky if we manage even a single vote at the next election.'

'It's a little more serious than your political career.'

'Yes. I . . . I suppose it is.'

'Then you can understand why I have taken some precautions.'

The Prime Minister looked confused. 'What kind of precautions?'

Felix ignored the question. 'I believe that the country might be on the brink of something even worse than you have imagined. Something catastrophic. Perhaps even anarchy –'

'*Anarchy?*' the Prime Minister furrowed his brow and repeated it again under his breath. 'How do you know all of this?'

'I have the resources.'

'Mr Felix, I can assure you I take all of this very seriously, but I don't believe for one moment that –'

'Within the next year there will be a march on Parliament.'

'I'm sure the police are more than capable of dealing with a few protesters, Mr Felix –'

'The police will be completely overwhelmed. The march will turn to rioting. The rioting will inevitably turn to massacres.' Felix held the Prime Minister's gaze. 'This will be unlike anything that has ever been seen before. The country is a ticking bomb, with a fuse that has been burning for years. Even a fool could see it.'

'And you're quite sure of this?'

'I'm a busy man, Prime Minister. I wouldn't waste my time on hunches and vague suspicions. It is only a matter of *when*.'

The Prime Minister seemed to pale.

'The public sees that things are getting worse,' Felix continued. 'Spiralling endlessly out of control. And they see you, and your government, as responsible.'

'There's so much outside of our control. We have no power over any of it. No one does . . .'

'It sounds to me as if you have already given up, Prime Minister.'

'They say that all it takes is a butterfly beating its wings to start a hurricane on the other side of the world. How do you suggest we control that, Mr Felix?'

'By clipping the butterfly's wing.'

'Controlling chaos? I'm starting to wonder if all that money has finally gone to your head.'

'We have a couple of ideas, Prime Minister.'

'We?'

'There are four of us – the four wealthiest in the country. And a fifth who – shall we say – doesn't care for the publicity. We have a very select membership.'

'What is this?'

'Think of it as a promise. You might call it a *pledge*, a pledge that we will get the country back on its feet. Back to what it once was.'

Before the Prime Minister had time to digest Felix's words, the car turned a corner and pulled up alongside the kerb. 'I believe this is your stop, Prime Minister. Do think about what I said.'

The Prime Minister squinted through the raindrops at the Georgian townhouse in front of him.

'I want to know one thing,' he said, turning to Felix. 'Why now?'

'Because this affects us too,' Felix replied. 'All of us. And because we are running out of time.'

5

After a miserable hour of morning chores, Alyn collected a bowl of watery soup and some bread and lowered himself into a chair in the far corner of the canteen. He watched the overspill of queuing inmates, shoving and squeezing to advance themselves further along the line.

He was finishing his soup when Jes appeared and dropped into the seat opposite his.

'There you are,' she said warmly, and leant to kiss him lightly on the cheek. 'I was so worried.'

He forced a smile. 'I'm fine.'

'So aren't you going to tell me what happened?'

'They were taking me down to see Adler. I made a run for it.' He pulled away, exhaling. 'My own stupid fault. I wasn't thinking.'

'How far did you get?'

'I got over the fence,' he lied.

Jes's eyes widened.

'I was sure I had it this time, Jes. I was so sure. You ever had that feeling when everything is going right?'

'Yeah, actually.'

'It was like that – like I didn't even have to think. Like everything was falling into place.'

'It's the furthest you've got – anyone's got.'

'Yet I'm still sitting here, aren't I?' Keen to change the subject, he added, 'I take it you saw my new cellmate? He made quite an entrance.'

'And quite an exit,' said Martin Adler, who had suddenly appeared beside their table. 'You should've seen the fear in his eyes when he realized he was surrounded. Some time in solitary might soften him up.'

'Why – are you worried that he might take out another two of your men?' Alyn said, without thinking.

The chief warden grabbed Alyn's grey uniform beneath the neck and hoisted him out of his chair. 'You're on thin ice, Hart.'

'Let go . . . I can't breathe.'

'There's nothing out there: nothing for you to run home to.'

'P-please,' Alyn croaked.

'We'll always find you, and we'll bring you straight back. You're here for a long time, Hart. You'd better get used to it.'

Adler threw Alyn back into his chair and scowled at Jes. 'What are you looking at?'

Jes quickly lowered her eyes to her meal, which now seemed distinctly unappetizing.

Adler frowned at the pair, and marched away to settle a dispute between two prisoners on the other side of the canteen.

Jes waited until he was out of earshot before speaking. 'I guess you must be pleased.'

'About what?'

'Well, with you and the new guy sharing a cell together . . .'

'What's that supposed to mean?'

'He seems like he won't want to stay put. With the pair of you working together, you might be able to –'

'I'm not doing another escape, Jes. I'm finished.' Alyn hadn't realized how much those words would hurt. 'I can't keep building my hopes up. I can't keep thinking it's ever going to happen.'

'So you'd rather spend your life in here? What *happened* to you, Alyn? What's changed?'

'Nothing's changed. And that's exactly the problem. How many times have I tried to break out now? I've lost count. And each time I never get any closer. I'm going nowhere.'

'You made it over the fence.'

Alyn wished he hadn't lied about his progress. *Had it been to impress her? To give her hope?*

'Adler's right – what difference would it make if I even made it into the forest? We don't know how long it goes on for; we don't even know *where* we are. We could be anywhere.'

Jes looked away. 'I can't believe I'm hearing this. When did you turn into such a cynic?'

'When I stopped believing in the impossible. Do you know how unlikely it is that any of us are ever going to see the outside world ever again? They need us here. I don't know why, but they aren't going to let us go without a fight.'

Jes slumped against her chair, unable to hide her disappointment. 'You've stopped dreaming, Alyn.'

'Maybe it's time we all stopped dreaming,' he said. 'It's never going to happen.'

'That's the point of a dream. Anything else is a compromise. I'm not giving up that easily. If you want to stay here, fine. But I'm getting out of here, one way or another.'

6

Ryan had been awake for several minutes. He blinked slowly, gazing at the strip of light beneath the door. Outside he could hear faint, muffled voices and the scrape of feet.

If I go back to sleep, he thought, *I might wake up and all of this will be a dream.* He closed his eyes.

'Ryan? *Ryan?* Were you even listening to a single thing I said?'

Ryan had been staring out of the car window at the surrounding houses, packed tightly together. Heaped in one of the gardens was a colourful pile of disused play things: plastic chairs and a broken tricycle. In another stood a washing machine with a missing door, scabbed with rust.

Ryan looked across at his friend, Carl, who was lounging with his feet up on the dashboard of his father's car. 'I spill me guts to you and you're too busy daydreaming. Never telling you anythin' ever again.'

'Give me the keys,' Ryan said, ignoring his friend. Carl tossed him the keys, which Ryan snatched out of the air.

'You promise you'll be careful. Dad'll kill me if there's as much as a scratch ...' Carl paused and removed his feet from the dashboard with a contemplative sigh. 'You ever think we're gonna get out of here?'

'Eh?'

'Here. This street. This city. Sheffield. Or do you think we'll just end up like our dads ...'

Ryan flinched.

'I'm sorry, mate. I didn't mean *your* old man, I just ...'

'I know. It's fine.' Ryan drummed his fingers on the steering wheel. 'I'm not gonna spend the rest of my life here in the middle of nowhere either. I want to do something with my life.'

The pair sat in silence for a few moments until Carl spotted a single figure in the rear-view mirror, ambling slowly towards them from round the corner. '*Damn*,' he hissed. 'Police!'

'Keep still,' Ryan said, and reached over to calm his friend. 'Don't draw attention to us.'

But by then it was too late. Carl fell out of the car quickly. Ryan shoved the door open, tumbled on to his side and scrambled to a crouch.

Carl scurried round the front of the car and sat with his back pressed against the bumper.

Ryan was about to follow him when he tripped over an empty bottle. The bottle clinked on the pavement.

The sound caught the policeman's attention. 'Oi!' he yelled, spotting Ryan sneaking away.

Ryan sprang up and sprinted across the pavement. The wind tore past his ears, and he felt his lungs heaving. The police officer's feet pounded on the pavement behind him.

'Carl!' He looked back over his shoulder. 'Carl, help –'

He sprang round the corner into an alleyway, crashing into a wall. He yelped and clutched his shoulder, turning the next corner only to find himself faced with a dead end.

'Got you!' the police officer panted as he closed in on him. 'Thought you'd go for a drive, did you?'

'I wasn't doing anything,' Ryan puffed. 'I swear it.'

'Tell that to the judge. Joyriding is a serious crime.' The officer removed his radio from his belt. 'Send some back-up. I've got a feeling this one isn't going quietly –'

There was a loud whooshing sound from behind him. The officer murmured and fell.

Ryan backed against the wall, staring at his fallen

pursuer, before turning his attention to the man who had emerged from the shadows.

The stranger stepped over the unconscious police officer. 'Ryan Farrell. We've been looking for you.'

Ryan exhaled and looked down at the barrel of the metal cylinder in the man's hands. 'Who are you? What did you do to him?'

Ryan had just started to doze when the door creaked open. He winced, shielding his eyes with his hand.

Tempted to launch himself at his captor, Ryan managed, somehow, to hold back. *That won't get me anywhere*, he thought. *This is their game. Their rules.*

'Could've given me some warning,' he muttered, clambering to a sitting position against the cold wall.

The teacher stepped inside. 'What you did yesterday was spectacularly stupid, Ryan.' She lowered herself down to be level with her prisoner. 'The wardens aren't happy. And neither are the people I answer to. They want you kept in solitary, at least for another few days.'

Ryan struggled to hide his alarm. 'Another few *days* . . . in here?'

'Mm-hm. Maybe even longer.'

She looked around the cell, nodding almost imperceptibly, like an architect furnishing the room in her imagination.

'It's small in here, isn't it? Small and dark. And you don't even have a pillow. Funny, isn't it, the things we take for granted? Like a pillow. Like *light*. How are you finding it in the dark?'

Ryan could feel his pulse quickening.

'You keep someone in the dark for too long and they start seeing things,' she continued. 'A mind needs to be kept active, or it starts creating its own entertainment. You have a mind that needs to be kept very active, don't you?'

'Who are you?' he hissed.

She answered his question with a distracted smile. 'With a click of my fingers I could have you taken back to your cell, with the others. It's better than nothing, don't you think? Certainly better than this.' She paused, making another brief survey of the room. 'But first I have to know that you have remorse: that you're sorry for what you've done and won't ever do it again. Just say the word and you'll be back in your cell.'

The thought of spending another minute in confinement filled Ryan with a steepening dread.

'Just tell me you're sorry, Ryan,' she continued. 'And everything will be forgiven.'

Ryan remained silent. His breathing was tense and shallow.

Do it, a voice inside him urged. *Tell them what they want. That you're guilty. Play their game.*

Ryan thought back to what Alyn had told him: that they would break him. It would start with a confession, then doubt, and then he wouldn't know who he was, or what he had done, and soon he would be nothing more than another broken cog in a strange machine.

'You had your chance,' the teacher said, and surrendered a disappointed sigh. 'Goodbye, Ryan.'

She turned to leave, but before she reached the door Ryan spoke. 'I'm sorry. I'm sorry for what I did.'

She paused and slowly pivoted on the heel of her shoe.

Ryan knew he had to get out if he wanted to stay sane. Already he could feel the edges of his world beginning to fray.

'I was angry,' he admitted, trying to swallow the lump in his throat. 'I didn't mean to do it – I wasn't thinking.'

The teacher smiled coolly. 'I think we're finally getting somewhere.'

'Hey, where are you going?' Ryan yelled as she walked away. 'You said all I –'

The door slammed closed behind her and soon Ryan's calls were barely a whimper, and then they were nothing at all.

7

Elsa Winchester tapped the door of the interrogation room. When no reply came she pushed it open.

A coffee stain had discoloured the desk and a patch of the concrete floor. She kicked aside the few jagged shards of a broken porcelain cup and reached across for her mop.

She'd seen plenty of escape attempts in the past – she'd even tried one or two herself – but this was the first time she'd heard of anyone actually *attacking* the guards. *If only I'd been there to see it . . .*

As she was sweeping the broken shards from under the desk, Elsa spotted something on the floor. A leather-bound folder.

The teacher must have dropped it. She picked it up and turned it over in her hands. It was unlike the teacher to leave anything lying around.

Elsa opened the folder but was halted by the sound of footsteps in the corridor. She shoved it inside her grey uniform just as the door swung open.

'It's time you finished up, Winchester. Get that stuff back to the store cupboard and head back to your cell.'

'Yes, sir.' Elsa picked up the bucket and scurried along, with the guard following her.

Once she was alone inside the cupboard, Elsa removed the file and stashed it behind a cardboard box. Whatever it was, it would have to wait until tomorrow.

On the way back to her cell, Elsa passed Julian, who was lounging on his mattress with his hands folded behind his head. *Looks like someone's enjoying skipping chores*, she thought, and wondered what he might've done to be allowed such a privilege.

'What are you looking so happy about?' she said.

He scowled at her. 'I'm thinking.'

'Yeah, well, don't hurt yourself. You've been smug ever since Alyn got caught.'

'It's called *Schadenfreude*.'

Elsa hated it when Julian used words she didn't know. The first few times she had asked him what they meant, but he always repelled her questions with a weary, deflated breath and a roll of the eyes, as if, at thirteen, she was just too ignorant to understand.

'It means taking pleasure from the misfortune of others,' Julian added, as though reading her mind.

'At least Alyn's doing something. I'd escape with him if I could.'

A thin smile spread across Julian's lips. 'You couldn't keep a secret if your life depended on it. You'd be blabbing to everyone in two minutes. No one would want to take you anywhere with them.'

'You're just jealous nobody wants to tell *you* any secrets. Nobody will ever trust you.'

For a moment, Elsa thought she saw a flicker of hurt in Julian's face but then he kicked his foot in her direction, as though shooing a dog. 'Go on,' he said. 'Get out of my sight.'

Elsa turned and silently walked away, but as soon as she was out of his sight she sprinted along the walkway to her cell.

Once in bed she used the zip on the front of her uniform to scratch a mark into the brick wall. *Three months,* she considered, quickly tallying the assortment of scratches, and closed her eyes.

'Mum and Dad don't trust me,' Elsa said, folding her arms as the train pulled away between the rows of houses. 'Otherwise why send you along?'

'Because you're only thirteen,' Simon answered. 'And I'm your big brother.'

'Bet they weren't like this with you.'

He raised his eyebrows. 'They were worse actually. What do you need to do again anyway?'

'Take some pictures. For this stupid art project. The theme is "hidden connections".'

Simon smiled sympathetically as Elsa slumped, resting her head on the window. He reached down, lifted up a discarded newspaper from the carriage floor and flicked through the crumpled pages. A photograph showed the businessman James Felix climbing into a car.

'The country is screwed and he has more money than he knows what to do with,' Simon commented. 'You should hear the kind of things they say about him. The rumours.'

'Yeah? Like what?'

'That he's part of some secret group that are trying to take over the world.'

Elsa lifted her head from the rattling window to look at the picture. 'He doesn't look all that powerful. He looks like Grandad.'

Simon shrugged. 'The world won't be taken over with guns and swords. It'll be with smiles and signatures.'

'Where did you hear that – one of those weird conspiracy books you're always reading?' She peered out of the window. 'Anyway, looks like it's our stop. Let's go.'

The pair went through the ticket barriers and down some steps to an empty car park. A plastic bag floated along, silently.

'So where do you want to go?' he said.

'I'm going to take some pictures around here.' She pulled her camera out of its case. 'I won't be long.'

'Stay in sight,' Simon commanded. He pulled himself up on to a wall by a ticket machine and started impatiently swinging his legs back and forth.

You're as bad as Mum and Dad, she thought and trotted away, aiming the camera at a solitary pigeon that was pecking around for crumbs.

After wandering for some time without finding much inspiration, Elsa looked back at her brother, who was still sitting over by the ticket machine, playing with his phone.

Still in sight. Technically. She followed some concrete steps down to a fenced area with an electricity box. Pinned to the wire was a metal sign:

CCTV SURVEILLANCE CAMERAS IN USE

Elsa took a photograph of it, then another of the indecipherable graffiti on the box beneath.

She looked at the camera screen and toggled back and forth between the image of the warning sign and the graffiti.

'You're not supposed to be down here.'

Elsa turned round. A man wearing a black jacket was watching her from the steps.

'Oh,' she said. 'I was just ...' She pointed to her camera. 'Taking some pictures for school.'

She started to jog up the stairs, but the man blocked her way. 'I can't let you leave, Elsa.'

Elsa backed away. 'How . . . how do you know my name?'

He took a step towards her. In his hand was a black cylinder. 'You're younger than I thought you'd be,' he said and pointed the object in her direction.

Elsa, baffled, raised her hands. 'Simon!' she called, switching her attention between the object and the man holding it.

'I mean . . . you're just a kid,' he went on. 'What are you, twelve? Thirteen?' The cylinder trembled in his hand.

'Simon!' Elsa called again, louder. '*Simon!*'

She let out a sudden cry and fell forward, unconscious.

A second man appeared from some way behind and lowered his weapon. 'What were you waiting for?' he growled at his colleague. 'Someone could've heard her.' He stopped beside the fallen girl then looked up, scowling. 'Hurry up and get her out of here.'

8

'You know what that means!' Adler yelled over the sound of the late-afternoon bell. '*Education.*'

A hundred teenage inmates collectively got to their feet as the cell doors rumbled open. There were three 'self-development' lessons each week: lessons that usually involved being forced to watch old, peculiar films on a projector that seemed several decades out of place.

'Don't look so miserable,' he continued. 'Some of you might even learn a thing or two.'

Alyn brushed his fringe out of his eyes and left his cell, reluctantly assimilating into the shuffling crowd. For some reason the lessons always gave him a headache, and if the body language of the others afterwards was anything to go by he wasn't the only one.

The line of inmates from the upper cells continued round the walkway and descended the staircase to where they joined the queue on the ground floor. Under the keen supervision of the wardens, they filed along the corridor, past the canteen to the classroom. Inside the dank, unpainted room were ten rows of individual wooden desks.

When the last inmate was seated, one of the younger guards marched over to the doors. He made a quick survey of the seated prisoners and joined his colleagues, who were huddled at the front of the room.

Alyn looked around and caught sight of Jes sitting on the next row. As if feeling his eyes on her, she glanced up. *Hey*, he mouthed, but she had already looked away.

The door opened and the teacher stepped through and stood at the front, between the guards. Her presence immediately caused the chatter in the room to cease.

'Speak,' she said.

'*We are prisoners because we are guilty,*' the inmates repeated in unison. '*We are guilty because we are flawed. We are flawed because we are human. We accept our guilt . . .*'

'Someone isn't co-operating,' said one of the guards, leaning in towards the teacher.

'Is that so?'

He pointed to a blonde girl, a few desks back from the front. '*Her*. Her lips were moving but she wasn't saying anything . . .'

The girl was pinned to the spot by a hundred pairs of eyes.

'You have nothing to say?'

'I'm – I'm not saying anything. Because I'm not guilty. I haven't done anything.'

The teacher studied her closely for several moments, then turned to the rest of the room. 'I assume you all heard that. This young lady claims she is innocent. Do you believe her?'

'*No*,' they said.

'You haven't fooled them,' she said, smirking. 'What makes you think you can fool me?'

'It's . . . it's been a week,' the girl stammered. 'And I'm not guilty. There's no way you can change my mind.'

'Actually, my dear, it's very easy to change a mind. Disappointingly easy.' She approached the girl's desk. Her pale fingers drifted absently through the girl's hair.

'It's rather simple, you see. We seek pleasure . . . and we flee from pain. If something becomes associated with pain, the mind takes refuge in something a little more . . . *convenient*.' She coiled a loop of the girl's blonde hair round her finger. 'You're guilty.'

'I'm innocent.'

She yanked hard on the hair. The girl cried out in pain and raised her hands to her head.

The teacher presented her hand to the girl. There were several strands of hair between her fingers.

45

'Such pretty hair. It would be a shame to lose it.' She released the hairs, which floated down gently to the floor. 'You're guilty,' she continued.

'No,' the girl said, shaking her head. 'I'm not guilty. I'm innocent . . .'

The teacher pulled the girl's hair again, tearing out another handful. The girl shuddered; her eyes filled with tears.

'You're guilty. Guilty, just like all the others.'

'I'm guilty,' the girl sobbed bitterly. 'Please, no more. No more . . . *I'm guilty.*'

The teacher brushed her fingertips to the ends of the girl's hair. 'That's right, child. For now you merely repeat it, but soon enough you'll believe it.' She patted her on the shoulder and smiled with almost maternal pride. The girl's sobs echoed in the silent room.

Alyn turned away to see Jes looking at him. She glanced down just as the lights dimmed and a projector bulb flickered to life.

'You're going to learn about economics,' the teacher said. 'We feel that some financial advice might stand you in good stead once you're released. Do you realize the kind of debt the country is in?'

Her question was met with silence from the assembly of blank, illuminated faces. 'You're quiet today. And I thought you always looked forward to my lessons.' She failed to subdue a sigh and slipped past the projector, her silhouette large and threatening for a couple of moments.

A steady crackle accompanied the film, which began to jump and warp violently as soon as it appeared. Alyn figured it must be a few decades old at least. *Guess they probably spent all their budget on their weapons,* he considered, crossing his arms tightly. *Then again, hasn't that always been the case?*

A succession of colourful benign diagrams appeared on the screen. None of the inmates, except a boy with glasses at the front of the room, noticed the corporate logo, which flashed up and disappeared after a split second. But before long even he put it down to being nothing more than a trick of the light.

9

The inmates were returning from the canteen after lunch the next day when a diminished-looking Ryan was marched back to his cell.

In just a couple of days, he seemed to have aged considerably: there were bags under his blue eyes, and his skin seemed almost as grey as his uniform. He sat on the edge of his mattress, and waited as the guards roughly removed his handcuffs.

'You try anything,' the taller of the guards said under his breath, tapping the ibis clipped to his belt.

'They made you confess, didn't they?' said Alyn, once the guards left the cell.

Ryan looked up at Alyn, but it seemed as though he was looking directly through him. 'They said they were going to leave me in there until I did. What choice did I have?'

'That's how they keep us compliant. They make us feel like we're broken. That we need to be fixed. It's all part of their game.'

'I'm not staying here,' Ryan said. 'I'm getting out of here if it kills me. Someone will find us . . . They'll send search parties out. They can't keep us here forever. They can't. There'll be people out there looking for us.'

'Not if whoever is behind this doesn't want us found,' said Alyn.

Ryan got to his feet and began pacing the cell. 'I could kill them. Every single one of them . . .'

'That won't solve anything.'

'Maybe it won't. But it'll make me feel better.'

Alyn wanted to smile, but couldn't summon the strength. He turned to find Jes watching them both.

'Can you blame him?' she said, coming in.

'This is Jes,' Alyn said. 'We're . . . friends.'

Ryan examined her for a few moments, and felt his anger quickly begin to subside. 'Hi,' he said.

'Jes is our conspiracy theorist,' Alyn explained. 'She's got quite an imagination. We've heard everything from this being some kind of experiment to a sick reality show.'

'*She* is still in the room. Anyway, I don't see you coming up with any better ideas. What are things like out there? It seemed like everything was falling apart last I saw . . .'

'They're saying things are starting to change. Depends whether or not you believe them.'

'Has there been anything about *us*? I mean, is anyone even looking for us?'

Ryan furrowed his brow, trying to remember if he'd seen her image in a newspaper. 'I don't know,' he finally said.

It wasn't the answer Jes wanted to hear. 'You don't remember? They've taken a hundred of us and you're telling me you're not even sure if people know we're missing?'

'There are a lot of missing teenagers,' Alyn interrupted. 'I mean, how many faces can *you* remember? If anything, people are just going to think we're runaways.'

'My friends won't,' said Jes. 'They know I would never have done something like that.'

'Mine too. But those are the voices nobody is going to hear –' said Alyn.

'You said something about escaping,' Ryan interrupted. 'Is it actually possible?'

'He made it over the fence just a couple of days ago,' Jes said proudly to Ryan. 'He's the first of us to do so.'

Alyn shrugged. 'I was so sure I had it that time.'

'What's out there?' Ryan said, peering out of the window.

'Past those trees? I have no idea. Nobody does.'

'How are you managing to escape the cell?'

'These are pretty old locks. They've already transferred me to five different cells . . .'

'A lock-picker. You sure you're really as innocent as you claim?'

Alyn frowned, which was a good enough answer as any.

'What about getting outside?'

'You could make a run for it during recess – it's pretty much the only freedom we have, but there are guards everywhere. You wouldn't last five minutes. Take it from me.'

'We need a plan,' Ryan said. 'We need to get out of here before we end up like all the others . . .'

Jes shot an accusing glance at Alyn. 'This is what I've been saying all along. No more going it alone.' She opened her mouth to say more but spotted Adler making his way towards them.

'Here comes trouble,' she said, and slipped out of the cell.

'You're looking pale, Farrell,' the chief warden said. 'Looks like you haven't seen the sun in days.' He laughed and whistled merrily to himself as he ambled along the walkway.

Escape, Ryan pondered, lying back on his mattress.

Escape. He muttered it under his breath, relishing the gentle hiss of the word. *Escape.*

Adler was already waiting by the office with his arms crossed when Julian appeared.

'Hello, Martin,' Julian said.

'I'd prefer it if you didn't get too familiar, Sleave. Remember, I'm the one in charge here. What have you got for me?'

'A question, actually.'

'A question? You know full well I'm not here to answer your questions. Have you forgotten that I'm the one with the key to your cell –'

'All right then,' Julian interrupted. 'No questions. How about we do a little exchange instead?'

Adler folded his arms more tightly and gave a permissive nod.

'It's about the boy in cell nine. Daniel something-or-other. Him and another boy are going to cause a diversion during morning recess. While everyone's occupied he's going to make a run for it.'

'Is there anyone who hasn't tried that?' Adler snorted, turning away. 'If you think you're getting anything in return, you must be kidding.'

'The diversion involves an attack. On one of the guards.'

Adler paused and slowly turned round to face Julian again.

'It's Ratchet,' Julian confirmed. 'They see him as the weakest guard.'

Adler stroked his chin. 'All right, Sleave,' he eventually said. 'What do you want?'

'No chores for the rest of the month. I watch the

others breaking their backs, and, well, I just don't feel like working.'

'That's one thing I like about you, Sleave,' Adler said with a gusty laugh and stomped along the corridor. 'You're scum, just like all the others. But at least you accept it.'

For your trust, I'll accept anything, Julian thought, watching him disappear from view.

Elsa shoved the mop in the bucket, sending soapy liquid spilling over the sides.

'Can I get some water?' she said to the guard, who was sitting on a chair a short way down the corridor. 'I haven't had anything to drink since this morning. I feel faint.'

The guard looked up at her and flicked idly through his magazine.

'I promise I'll be quick.'

'You'd better be, Winchester. If you're not back in two minutes, I'll have you cleaning toilets for the rest of the year. Understood?'

Elsa leant the mop against the wall, then ran down the corridor. Rather than turning right for the drinking fountain, she darted inside the store cupboard and closed the door behind her. She lowered herself to her knees and reached behind the box for the leather folder. She opened it and pulled out a document, turning to the first page. Bold black letters stated:

THE ABILITY

'*The Ability?*' Elsa read aloud quietly, squinting at the words. She sat herself down on a box and thumbed through the pages.

... Studies suggest that the Ability is most prominent from eight to eighteen. On reaching adulthood there appears to be a marked decrease, although there are, of course, some adults who still exhibit particular tendencies. As has been acknowledged by some researchers, the Ability is like a 'muscle' that gets weaker if it is not utilized ... it appears to be non-conscious involvement that is the active mechanism ...

... A random number generator is seemingly affected by presence alone and is, at this point in time, the clearest measure of Ability ... effects are dramatically increased when one or more subjects are together in a particular location ... the mechanism remains unknown ... comparisons have been drawn with chaos theory; the setting in motion of a chain of events ... appears to operate through the realms of chance ...

... Most effective methods for harnessing the Ability have been shown to be symbolism and symbolic enactment, necessity and a mental 'sleight of hand' – in the latter, subliminal images are flashed repeatedly at the subjects, bypassing conscious awareness ... the Pledge has suggested that problematic subjects may benefit from being confined to an isolated area of reduced variables ... cost is, as expected, not an issue ...

'This doesn't make any sense,' Elsa muttered, trying her best to decipher the streams of tightly packed prose. It was as she turned the page that her mouth fell open.

10

Six months ago

Harlan pushed through the press of commuters. The rain was fizzling across the pavement, crashing against the windscreens of congested traffic. The tarpaulin sheath of a flower stall beside the train station rattled and flapped furiously in the wind.

Glad to be out of the storm, Harlan found a spot by the entrance. He was brushing the rain from his jumper when he felt someone approach him.

'You must be Harlan.'

He looked up to find himself facing a white-haired, bearded man wearing a long tattered overcoat.

'I didn't think you were going to show,' he said. 'Come, let's find somewhere we can talk.'

'Wait a minute, aren't you going to tell me your name?' Harlan said.

The man's eyes flitted over Harlan cautiously. 'When I can be sure I trust you.'

Ten minutes later, the pair were sitting at the back of a coffee shop, some way down a quiet street. 'So,' the man said, pushing his polystyrene cup to one side. 'I want to know how you found me.'

'I looked online – for others like me. I stumbled across your website. It looked like it hadn't been updated in years, but there was a contact email at the bottom of the page. I wasn't really expecting a reply. Weeks passed and I forgot about the whole thing. Then a couple of months later I got your response so here I am – to "discuss things", as we agreed.'

The man turned his eyes to the window momentarily, nodding to himself as though verifying Harlan's story. 'My name's Henry,' he said.

'Is that really your name, or are you trying to make me think you trust me?'

Henry smiled. 'You're a smart boy, Harlan. Tell me how things are for you at the moment.'

'You mean school, or –'

'You know exactly what I mean.'

Harlan looked at the table. 'It's been getting worse since I wrote to you. The coincidences are everywhere ... It feels ... it feels like I'm going mad. Or that I already am.'

'Perhaps you are.'

'I began to see patterns everywhere, in everything. Things that were totally separate ended up connected ... I would think about someone I hadn't seen in a year and later that day I'd bump into them ... I'd walk into shops and know what songs were going to be playing ... I would know things I shouldn't. Even my friends started to notice ...'

'And?'

'And it's still happening ... more than ever – there must be a way to make it stop.'

'I can't make it stop,' Henry said. 'But you aren't alone. There are others like you.'

'Where? I have to meet them.'

'Not yet, Harlan.'

Henry took a sip from his cup, but halted suddenly and looked out of the window. The rain had all but ceased.

'What's wrong?' Harlan asked.

'Nothing.' Henry pushed the cup to one side and quickly got to his feet. 'I have to go. I'll be in touch soon.'

'You can't just leave – I have more questions ...' Harlan tried to grab his arm, but Henry pulled away and removed a silver coin from his pocket.

'Practice,' he whispered, flipping the coin towards Harlan and making his way out of the cafe.

'Wait! You haven't told me why –'

Harlan hurried after him but bumped into a girl carrying a tray of drinks. The girl gasped as the drinks hit the floor.

'I'm sorry!' Harlan said, exhaling. He snatched a

few napkins from the counter, threw them at her, then sped out of the coffee shop, looking left and right.

Harlan thought he saw Henry disappear round a corner. He gave chase, dodging past a few ambling pedestrians, turned the corner and ran into an alleyway. It was a dead end.

'Hey, kid.'

Harlan looked over his shoulder. A couple of men dressed in black were walking towards him.

'You lost or something?'

'I'm looking for someone,' Harlan panted, and tried pushing past them back the way he had come.

'That's funny,' the smaller of the men said, 'cos we were looking for someone too. And we just found him.'

Harlan pulled his outdoor coat tighter. The snow creaked and crunched underfoot as he walked across the rectangular exercise yard. A group of boys were chasing after a ball in the centre court. A warden either side prevented the inmates from drifting round the corners of the prison.

He linked his fingers around the wire fence, staring at the crooked, bare trees beyond.

'Are you Harlan?'

The voice jolted Harlan from his trance.

'Apparently you "know things",' Ryan continued. Flecks of snow were melting in his curly hair. 'Why don't you fill me in?'

Harlan turned round. 'I know you've already tried to escape. I know your name is Ryan.'

'I didn't mean about me. I meant about *here*.'

Harlan's gaze came to rest on the fence again. 'I have feelings. Intuitions,' he said. 'You look disappointed.'

Ryan sighed and shoved his hands in his pockets. 'I heard a rumour that you were digging through your cell wall.'

'There are lots of rumours here.'

'You don't have to be vague with me, Harlan. I've not been *turned* or anything.'

'It's not you I'm worried about,' Harlan said, noticing Julian loitering just metres away from them. He indicated for Ryan to come to the fence and said, 'You need to be careful of him. His name's Julian. If he has any idea that I'm digging –'

'*Are* you digging?'

Harlan's voice fell to a whisper. 'There's talk of a tunnel somewhere in the prison. Another rumour, of course. But one that's been floating around since we got here.'

'And what makes you think you can get to it?'

'The same thing that makes anyone think they'll be led somewhere: hope.' Harlan studied Ryan intently. 'You've thought it too, haven't you?'

'Thought what?'

'That you're different. That *we're* different.'

'You've lost me.'

'We've been asking the wrong questions,' Harlan went on. 'They've distracted us all with this ... this *prison*. But it's all a lie – an illusion. That's how magic works: you get someone to look in the wrong place, and you pull off the trick. Right in front of them.'

A baffled Ryan watched Harlan walk across the yard, shielding his eyes from the falling snowflakes.

'*Exercise is over!*' yelled one of the guards by the yard door, firing the ibis skywards. 'Get back inside!'

Harlan waited until it was lights out before crawling under the bed to resume his work on the wall.

Except for a coughing boy a few cells away, all was silent, and it was so cold that he could see wisps of breath. Shivering, Harlan angled the silver coin between his fingers and began lightly scraping at the cement.

How the others could just sit there and do nothing baffled him. Did they not care whether or not they were rescued? Were they still holding out the hope that someone might find them? He had been here too long for that and it was clear that nobody was coming.

11

Two years ago

Felix was standing with his back against the low wall, arms wrapped defiantly against the slicing winds. He watched the commuters pour silently across the bridge, organizing themselves like traffic into lanes of fast and slow.

'I assume you've spoken with the Prime Minister, Felix?'

'Emmanuel,' said Felix, looking up. 'It's good to see you.'

Although the pair had been acquainted for over a year, Felix still knew next to nothing about his suited adviser. Even his name was almost certainly an alias.

'Well?'

'He took some persuading, but I got there in the end. He agreed. All that we have left to do is to acquire the children. I think I might have found a suitable location.'

Felix removed a creased photograph from his coat pocket. 'A derelict factory in the Scottish highlands. Surrounded by miles of woodland. I'm sure it could be adapted for our purpose, don't you think?'

Emmanuel took the photograph in his gloved hand and studied it for a couple of seconds.

'It's in the middle of nowhere,' Felix added. 'I have it on good authority that the winters are fierce.'

'All the more reason for them to stay put.'

'My thoughts entirely. What about our candidates? Is there any news?'

'Susannah Dion, the psychologist, has the list. There are a hundred, as we discussed.'

Felix shivered as an icy wind swept by. 'There is one nagging concern I have about all of this. The facility itself. How can we provide a suitable cover story for the guards?'

'We tell them that it's a prison. For young offenders. With the necessary forgeries it will be a convincing illusion.'

'What if they suspect something is going on?'

'What could they possibly suspect? As long as they're paid well enough they won't suspect a thing.'

'I – I don't know,' Felix said, scratching his temple. 'It just all seems a bit . . .'

'Cunning?'

'Cruel.'

'They will need to be broken.' Emmanuel rested his

elbows on the wall overlooking the river. His overcoat flapped round his calves. 'To break them, we will need to make them doubt themselves. To make them doubt themselves, we will need to make them feel guilt. There can be no other way. I hope you're not having second thoughts.'

'No, I –'

Emmanuel's eyes were unblinking. 'We've come too far. I won't have you lose your nerve now, Felix.'

'I'm – I'm not losing my nerve. I will have a team put together at once. And I want the facility ready as soon as possible. The longer we delay, the worse it will be . . . for everyone.'

Emmanuel watched Felix closely, like a predator searching for a sign of weakness in its prey. 'That is why we are doing this, isn't it? For the greater good. You should never lose sight of that.'

'For the greater good,' Felix repeated. *And ourselves*, he very nearly added, but managed to hold his tongue. *And ourselves.*

12

After his talk with Harlan, Ryan returned to his cell while the inmates milled around for recess. He followed the walkway to find Jes sitting cross-legged on Alyn's bed.

'I see they had you sweeping snow out there,' he said. 'You in trouble or something?'

'Oh, that? That's my usual job,' she muttered. 'Seemed like a good idea when the weather was better. Now it's winter I'm not so sure. So what chores have they given you?'

'What *haven't* they given me?' He kicked off his boots. 'Wash room in the morning, cleaning in the afternoon. They're even threatening a load of other stuff too.'

'Guess it's a waste of breath to ask how you're finding it here then,' Jes answered.

Ryan cut his eyes around the cell. 'I've been in better. Part of me is still expecting to wake up.'

'You'd better get used to that.'

Ryan sat down on his bed. 'So I guess you're innocent as well?'

'Did you even need to ask?'

'Sorry.' He grinned. 'I mean you don't *look* like a criminal. Well, not much like one anyway.'

'Not much? I guess I'll take that as a compliment.'

He lay back and put his arms behind his head. 'I know it sounds crazy, but have you ever thought that they might be doing us all a favour?'

'Nope. Explain.'

'Well,' Ryan said. 'Things have been going pretty bad these past few years, haven't they ...? Maybe there's been some kind of war and they've gathered us all up so we can start over again.'

'Wait until Alyn hears that. He won't ever make fun of my theories again. Why would they want *us*?'

'Maybe because we're the smartest. Or the most upstanding ... or the best looking,' he said, briefly catching Jes's eyes. 'It doesn't matter. What is it with you and Alyn anyway? Are you together or something?'

'We're just friends.'

'And whose decision was that?'

'It was mutual.'

Ryan could see in her eyes a faint flicker of regret. 'I take it you haven't seen him around then. I wanted a word myself.'

'What about?' Jes asked, then immediately added, 'I'm sorry. It's none of my business.'

'It's fine. Alyn seems to know the ins and outs of this place better than anyone. I've been asking around, but –'

'You need to be careful. Not everyone here is trustworthy.' Jes lowered her voice. 'But if you want a way out there might be something; we've been looking for a tunnel.'

'The same tunnel Harlan seems to think he can get to through the wall in his cell? You don't seem convinced.'

'Even if Harlan's right, you know who's on the other side of that wall? *Julian*. If he has even the faintest idea that something's going on, he'll run straight to the guards.'

'Then we need to find a way to shut him up.'

Jes smiled. 'That's the kind of thing I've been waiting to hear.'

'I'm not giving up, Jes. I don't know what's going on – as far as I can see it's one lie after another. It's hard to know where one ends and another begins. *Nothing is true . . .*'

'Except?'

'Except that I'm getting out of here. *We're* getting out of here.'

'You want to be careful of this one, Farrell,' said Martin Adler, who suddenly appeared at the bars of the cell. 'Leave anything valuable lying around and it might end up missing.'

Jes's cheeks turned pink.

'We call her the magpie,' the chief warden continued, walking in. 'Seven burglaries in a month, would you believe? It's a good job we caught her when we did. Who knows what she might've done.'

Jes bit down on her lip and muttered something under her breath.

'What was that?' Adler probed. 'I'll hope you were expressing your gratitude. Go on, let's hear it. Say "thank you, sir".'

Jes was silent.

Adler removed his ibis from his belt and patted it menacingly with his gloved hand.

'Thank you . . . *sir*.' The words tasted bitter in her mouth.

'You're learning. You never know, by the time you finish in here you might even end up a decent member of society. But then again . . .'

Adler turned and marched merrily out of the cell. Jes caught Ryan's eyes for the briefest of moments before hurrying away herself.

Adler left the hall and had just entered the corridor when a distinctly panicked guard appeared from below, wiping his brow.

'Sir,' he said in a lowered voice. 'One of the inmates is missing.'

Adler froze mid-step. 'If it's Hart again, I swear I'll –'

'It's not Hart, sir. It's Elsa. Elsa Winchester. She hasn't been seen since she was on corridor duty –'

'The brat? She won't have got far. Lock down the cells. No one's to leave until she's found.'

'Sir,' he replied and raced across the hall, gesturing to the inmates. 'Get back inside your cells! Recess is over!'

'What's going on?' Jes said from her mattress, watching Adler summon two other wardens and leave with them through the double doors. After being in the facility as long as she had, it was easy to tell when something was afoot: the hiss of whispers, the sudden scuffle of boot steps on the concrete. She sat up straight, half expecting to see Ryan making another frantic dash for freedom.

'It's Elsa,' said Charlotte, Jes's cellmate.

Elsa? What's she playing at? Jes didn't bother waiting for her cellmate to elaborate and hurried over to the bars of her cell.

'Sit back down. Remember what happened the last time you tried getting involved?'

Jes didn't need reminding and felt herself wince at the thought of another ibis blast.

'We're all guilty. We must all take responsibility for what we've done,' Charlotte said, almost like she was reciting a mantra.

Jes looked at her, and felt a chill down her spine. 'You're delusional.'

'Am I?' Charlotte looked at her with glazed eyes. 'I was like you once: refusing to accept what I had done. I feel sorry for you.'

Jes was tempted to argue, but realized it was futile. She had seen too many of them turned, and once they accepted their guilt they were lost, almost cult-like, and their ability to reason seemed to disappear altogether. With a sigh, she miserably flopped back on to her mattress.

Elsa was so engrossed in the document that she didn't even realize Adler had opened the door to the stock cupboard. She panicked and hid the papers behind her back.

'Get up,' Adler snarled, grabbing her uniform and hoisting her to her feet. 'Thought you could skip work? You've had the whole prison looking for you, Winchester.'

'I – I'm sorry,' Elsa stammered as Adler launched her out of the cupboard. 'I was just tired –'

'How about a week in solitary? Plenty of time for you to catch up on your sleep . . .'

'No,' she begged. 'It won't happen again, I promise.'

Adler paused. His eyes travelled over her suspiciously. 'What have you got there?'

'Nothing . . .'

He spun her round and snatched the document out

of her hands. He thumbed through a few pages. 'Where did you find this?'

Elsa opened her mouth but found her words tying in knots.

'I said, *Where did you –*'

'The corridor. I – I found it in the corridor.'

'The corridor,' Adler repeated, disbelieving. He flicked to the last page and rolled the papers into a cylinder. 'How much of it did you read?'

'Not much. Honestly.'

Adler held her in his eyes, unblinking.

'All of it,' Elsa eventually confessed under his gaze. 'You people are crazy! You really believe this stuff?'

'We don't just believe it,' Adler said. 'We know it. We've seen it work. I don't expect you to understand. You're just a child.'

'I understand,' she said. 'And I'm going to tell the others. I'm going to tell everyone!'

Adler held the ibis just inches away from her forehead and pressed the trigger. Elsa crumpled to the floor.

'I'm sure you would, if you could remember,' he said.

13

As everyone was marching dolefully towards the classroom, Jes, some way at the back of the line, spotted Adler and another guard out of the corner of her eye. In between the pair was Elsa, being dragged along by her arms and legs.

'So you found her in the cupboard,' she heard the guard say. 'What do you think she was doing in there?'

'Nothing,' Adler grumbled. He checked that the rolled-up document in his back pocket hadn't fallen out.

'You don't think she was looking for that vent, do you, boss?'

'Maybe she was,' Adler lied. 'Let's just hurry up and get her back to her cell. I've got things to do.'

The guard nodded, picked up his pace and soon the trio disappeared round the corner.

A vent in the cupboard, Jes thought.

'Get inside,' came a voice from behind her. A guard shoved her hard and she stumbled into the classroom.

'They caught Elsa,' Jes murmured to Ryan as they sat at desks towards the back of the room.

'Too bad. I hope she doesn't get put in solitary.'

Jes leant her elbow on the desk and covered her mouth with her hand. 'I heard the guards say something interesting just now. I'll tell you about it later.'

'Tell him what?'

Jes hadn't noticed Alyn sitting behind them. She looked at him over her shoulder. 'Don't worry,' she said. 'You wouldn't be interested anyway. Not now . . .'

Alyn folded his arms tightly. 'If you two are planning something, I –'

Jes turned to the front of the room as the teacher entered. 'Just leave it, Alyn.'

'What is this anyway?' Ryan whispered.

'If you know what's good for you, you'll play along,' Jes whispered. '*I mean it.*'

Ryan reluctantly repeated the confession when they were prompted, and watched along with everyone else as the projector screen rolled down.

It was almost five minutes into the film when Jes noticed the frame: a single, split-second image showing a policeman with a baton raised against a group of rioters, who were spilling out from behind a barricade. Puzzled by what she had seen, in a film about moral development, Jes slowly sat up taller in her chair.

It's an old projector reel, she considered, trying to rationalize it, at the same time looking around to see if anyone else had noticed.

But less than a minute later there was another flash, showing a similar scene of a burning car surrounded by an angry mob.

'Did you see that?' she whispered to Ryan. Her eyes, still tethered to the screen, glistened in the low light.

'See what?'

'Those pictures. It's like they've been spliced into the film or something. It's the first time I've noticed them . . .'

'Didn't see anything.' He yawned.

'*No talking at the back!*'

Jes swept her hair out of her eyes and settled back in her seat. She didn't notice another picture for the rest of the film, and by the time it had finished she had almost forgotten about them.

The next morning, Jes peered into Elsa's cell as the inmates were being herded out of the hall for breakfast. Elsa was lying haphazardly across her mattress like a broken marionette. She grumbled, trying to move, but finding it a considerable effort.

'It was brave of you to try an escape,' said Jes, leaning against the bars. 'I'm impressed.'

'I wasn't trying to escape . . .'

'The guards thought otherwise.'

With some effort, Elsa managed to drag herself into a sitting position. Since recovering from the ibis blast, her mind felt muddled, but she could remember enough from before to know she hadn't tried to escape. *Why did they use an ibis on me?*

'It's not the first time they've been wrong, is it?' she said.

'No, it isn't the first time. And it won't be the last.' Jes forced a smile and stepped inside the cell.

'Do you think our parents are even looking for us? I mean, I thought someone would have found us by now . . .'

'They're looking for us. I know they are.'

'But?'

'But, for all we know, they're looking in the wrong place.'

Elsa lowered her eyes. 'If this is some kind of conspiracy, Simon will know about it. He believes in all that stuff.'

'Simon is your brother?'

'Yeah. He's eighteen.'

'Do you miss him?'

Elsa's eyes had glazed a little. She nodded absently. 'Though I'd never tell him that.'

She dragged herself weakly to her feet and was

passing Jes when she leant in close. 'I wasn't trying to escape, I swear it. But I have this really strange feeling that I discovered something. Something important. I wish I could remember . . .'

Before Jes could say anything back, Elsa withdrew into the throng and was soon lost among the jumble of grey uniforms.

14

First came the sound of breaking glass, then cheering, jeers and shouts. The crowd charged together across the street.

Simon Winchester got up from his computer desk and walked to the window. There were at least fifty rioters trickling in between the cars, most of them hooded with scarves covering their mouths. '*Jesus*,' he whispered, and ran downstairs. 'Mum, get away from the window!'

His mother, a short, curly-haired woman, was holding a photograph of her daughter, Elsa.

'Mum? Did you hear me?'

'I heard you.' She placed the photograph back on the cabinet and looked out of the window in a daze.

Simon had just pulled her to one side when the window exploded, showering the room with glass. A brick sailed past and crashed into the wall.

'What's going on? What are they doing?'

'The riots are breaking out everywhere,' Simon said. 'Have you not seen the news?'

'No.'

He sped into the hall and made sure the front door was double-locked. Through the peephole he could see the crowd surging into the road, a short way past the house.

'They started last night,' he called back to her. 'There was a protest in London, in the financial district. I hope Dad's all right . . .'

There was another crash and clatter of falling glass, then the piercing, pulsating shriek of a car alarm.

Simon went back into the kitchen, where his mother was sitting with her head drooped, and sat opposite her.

'This is the first time I've felt anything . . . since Elsa . . . the first time I've felt anything at all in three months and it took a brick through the window.' She tried to smile. Her face was hot with tears. 'Maybe it's for the best that she missed all of this. Things aren't going to get any better, are they?'

Simon lowered his eyes. 'You speak about her like she's dead.'

His mother blew her nose and rolled the tissue tightly into a ball.

'She's not dead,' he went on. 'I know she isn't. Can't you feel it?'

'No, Simon. I can't.'

'The number of children who have gone missing in the last year or so. It's . . . it's not normal. You even said yourself . . .'

'I said a lot of things. We all did.' She looked away. 'You don't still believe in all that conspiracy nonsense, do you?'

'You should look on the internet . . . you'll see there are plenty of things . . . People who've said they've seen men in vans taking kids . . . They think the government might even be involved.'

'They always think the government's involved. I'm sure they have enough on their hands. What good reason would they have to take people's children?' she snapped, suddenly composed again.

Simon paused, letting a few moments' silence fall. 'Do you hear that?' he eventually said.

'I don't hear anything, Simon.'

'Exactly. The rioting – it's stopped.' Simon got out of his chair and walked into the hall.

'Look,' he said, squinting through the peephole. 'People are just walking away.'

His mother walked cautiously into the living room. A stream of air was blowing fiercely through the broken window. She stepped over the shattered glass and gazed out on to the street. 'It's like they've all given up,' she pondered, watching a youth toss a rock on to the lawn and hurry away. 'Maybe they finally came to their senses.'

She pulled her cardigan tighter, shivering, and made her way back across the living room. Two plates had fallen from the cabinet and were lying in ruins on the floor; the only thing unscathed was the photograph of Elsa, which stood just inches from where the brick had struck.

'What's the matter?' Ryan asked, looking over at Alyn. 'You not speaking to me or something?'

'I know you've been trying to get Jes involved in your stupid escape plan,' he said.

'Ah. She told you.' Ryan looked disappointed for a split second. 'She's a big girl. She can do what she wants.'

'I don't want her going with you. You hadn't even been here an hour and you managed to get yourself put in solitary.'

'I learned my lesson. I'm a fast learner, me.'

'You're a loose cannon.'

Ryan snorted dismissively and stood up, stretching. He opened his eyes to find himself slammed back suddenly into the cell bars.

'What the hell are you doing?'

'Find Jes and tell her that you've changed your mind. I want you to leave her out of this.'

Ryan grabbed Alyn's hand and effortlessly wrenched it free.

'If you have a problem with me and Jes working together, you know where to find her,' Ryan said, brushing the creases out of his uniform.

'And I know where to find you. Remember that.'

Claude Rayner weighed up Julian with a glance, then walked back over to the table at the far end of the guards' room.

Steam was swirling from the plastic coffee cups on the table. Outside, the midday snowfall had petered out to a hazy rain. Julian watched the writhing raindrops clumsily descend the glass.

'Julian Sleave,' said one warden, who was standing by the sink. He slowly folded his arms. 'To what do we owe the pleasure?'

A couple of guards at the table sniggered. Julian sauntered across the room and pulled out one of the chairs.

'You just make yourself right at home,' said Rayner sarcastically. 'This'd better be good.'

Julian crossed his legs and folded his arms behind his head. 'I want to see Martin Adler. I have some information he might like to hear. Where is he?'

'He's not here. You'll have to make do with us instead.'

'In that case, I think I'll have a coffee. Milk, two sugars.'

The guards shared a look. Rayner swiftly drew his ibis. 'You've got exactly one minute to explain yourself.' He shoved it against Julian's temple.

'I won't need that long.' Julian glanced at the ibis admiringly. 'This truly is a remarkable creation, most probably the first of its kind. Who'd have thought that you, of all people, would have access to such advanced sonic weaponry? Makes me wonder how deep this whole thing goes. And, more importantly, who's funding it . . .'

Julian peered at the angry faces, which were watching his every move. 'I suppose the real selling point is that you can put someone in a lot of pain without even leaving a bruise. You could say it's weaponry for people who want to fight clean.'

Rayner's finger hovered over the trigger.

'But *I* prefer to think of it as weaponry for people who don't want to get their hands dirty.'

Rayner was unimpressed. 'You're running out of time, Sleave.'

Julian moved his trembling hands underneath the table. 'Your guess is probably as good as mine as to the long-term effects of the weapon but, having been on the receiving end of one, I can confirm that the short-term effects include acute pain, disorientation, nausea, lethargy, breathlessness, blackouts . . .'

'Ten seconds.'

'. . . and *amnesia*.' Julian looked at the ibis, which had still not been lowered, with a raised eyebrow. 'You still don't get it, do you?'

'Five seconds.'

Julian sighed. 'How can I give Martin Adler information if I can't remember it?'

Only then did Rayner understand, and reluctantly withdrew the weapon from Julian's forehead.

'We got there in the end, and it only took one minute,' Julian said, and glanced at the clock. 'Now how about that coffee?'

15

The day ticked by slowly for Jes, who was occupying herself with thoughts of escape. Ryan seemed serious about the whole thing; maybe he was just what they needed. She was too used to seeing inmates give up and accept crimes that they hadn't committed – crimes that, in many cases, they wouldn't even have considered committing. The lie spread through the prison like a plague, a disease, and she couldn't help but think that sooner or later it might claim all of them.

Who would be next? Elsa had had a vague, defeated look in her eyes the last time they spoke. Harlan was always quiet but had seemed even more distant than usual when she had seen him sitting in his cell, absurdly flipping a coin over and over.

Her thoughts trailed off as she idly watched the guards marching obediently around the upper level. Did they even realize what they were doing?

Jes recalled one guard who started working at the facility not long after she had been brought in. He had seemed just as baffled by it as she was. '*I've worked in prisons for the last twenty years,*' she had heard him saying to Martin Adler in the canteen one morning. '*But this is different. Something just doesn't feel right.*'

Not long after that conversation, the man was gone. He'd been offered a job elsewhere, apparently, although Jes found his sudden disappearance more than a little disconcerting.

'I want to speak to you about something,' Jes said as Ryan ambled past her cell, dragging a mop along behind him. 'Have you got a minute?'

Ryan shook his head. 'They've put me on cleaning duty. I'm already running late as it is.'

Jes leant against the locked cell door. 'I won't be long . . . I just need to talk to you. Are you still in?'

'I've been thinking about that,' Ryan said. 'Maybe it's not such a good idea. I've only been here five minutes . . .'

'You're starting to sound like Alyn.' Jes stepped away from the bars. 'He hasn't said anything to you, has he?'

'I've got to go . . .'

'I'll kill him,' she said under her breath.

'*Farrell!*' cried the guard from the ground floor. '*Quit dawdling and get down here.*'

Ryan offered Jes a sympathetic smile and set off down the stairs.

'We need to talk,' Jes said to Alyn, who was standing beside Harlan in the lunchtime queue.

Harlan glanced at Jes and stepped away.

'What do you think you're playing at?' she asked.

Alyn looked at her blankly. 'I don't know what you're talking about.'

'You know exactly what I'm talking about.'

'Wait a minute, you mean this thing Ryan's trying to organize? How long has he been here? A few days?' Alyn looked around the canteen to make sure there were no guards listening. 'He has no idea what he's getting himself into.'

'At least he's trying. At least he hasn't given up.'

'He's still new. Give him time.' Alyn turned away but was spun back round by Jes.

'You're happy for us to stay like this forever?' she hissed, her whispers growing desperate.

'No. But we don't have any choice. No one's coming for us. No one has any idea where we are. Not our families, not the police. No one. Not even ourselves! And you know something? Ryan reminds me of how I used to be. Angry, obsessed. There's no use fighting any more. It took a while but I realized it. And so will he. So will everyone.'

He reached out to touch her, but Jes swatted his hand away.

'And someday,' he said, 'so will you.'

Ryan shoved the mop into the bucket and made his way down the corridor, wiping a film of sweat from his forehead.

'Where do you think you're going?' said the guard, who was leaning against the wall with his arms folded.

'Getting some water. You've had me doing this for hours. How much more do you want?'

'All right, Farrell, but be quick. You've still not finished.'

Ryan walked over to the drinking fountain and angled his mouth towards the paltry stream of water. He watched the guard until he turned to talk to one of his colleagues, then quietly slipped away.

Ryan sneaked round the corner and used the pen he had stolen from Alyn to make a brief sketch of the floor plan on the back of some paper towels.

Half-crouching, he neared a window that revealed the side of the prison. An adjacent corridor led through to the canteen.

Ryan examined the fence and the distance and height of the guard tower and made the necessary additions to the sketch. The lookouts seemed to be posted up there continuously. By the time anyone even thought about making a move towards the fence, everyone in the prison would know about it. And there was the small point of making it over the top . . .

'I thought you were supposed to be getting a drink, Farrell?'

Ryan stood up straight, hiding the paper towel and pen in his pocket. 'I was,' he said, trying to think of an excuse. 'I just . . .'

'Just nothing.' The warden grabbed Ryan by the collar and marched him back to the mop and bucket.

'I want this entire corridor so shiny I can see my face in it. And there's no point in you looking at that fence,' he said with a snarl. 'You're going nowhere.'

16

Alyn sat on the bench and began making idle patterns in the snow with the heel of his boot.

He gazed at the guard tower, watching as the huddled lookout rocked back and forth on the balls of his feet, trying to stir some warmth into his legs. The wire fence trembled gently in the wind, cradled by a creeping mist.

His memory of that night, a year ago now, was patchy and incomplete. But he remembered it had started with his father . . .

'So where are you taking me again?'

Alyn's father put the cigarette to his lips, then opened the car window to let some air in. 'The club. You can meet some of the guys. My friends. They're a rowdy bunch but they're all right.' His father smiled, revealing a crescent of yellowing teeth. 'I've been out of your life long enough. Thought I'd give you a glimpse of mine.'

I'd rather you took an interest in mine, Alyn thought, but smiled back anyway.

They soon arrived at a rundown-looking pub, with a boarded window. Two men stood outside, eyeing the car suspiciously.

'This it?' Alyn said, looking at the building with some concern.

His father nodded, pulling the cigarette from his lips and flicking it to the pavement.

They went in. The pub, almost empty, was filled with the familiar, sticky-sweet scent of beer.

'In here.' Alyn's father steered him further inside with a firm hand on his shoulder.

At the back of the pub was a group of about half a dozen men huddled round a table. One of the group was dealing playing cards.

Alyn's father pulled off his leather jacket and flung it into a heap on one of the empty tables at the side. 'Grab a seat.'

Alyn pulled over a chair and was about to sit, but his father dropped into it instead, and pulled himself close to the table.

A waft of cigarette smoke drifted into Alyn's face and he grimaced and looked down. A scrawny man with blurry, faded tattoos on his hands was smoking and watching him. 'How'd your old man drag you here? Tell you that you were going to Disneyland or something?'

'He's my good-luck charm – isn't that right?' Alyn's father removed a twenty-pound note from his pocket, tossing it into the middle of the table with several others.

'You want in?' the dealer said, looking at Alyn with a card poised.

'No,' his father quickly said. 'He's not playing. He doesn't even know how.'

'I could learn . . .'

His father looked up at him. 'I said *no.*'

Alyn folded his arms and stole a look at the clock. It was going to be a long night.

An hour passed, then two. His father amassed a small fortune of winnings, which was now a considerable bulge in his shirt pocket. A white-haired man in a grey overcoat had joined the group a short while ago, but had barely said a word to any of them.

'I'm going to get some fresh air,' Alyn said.

His father tossed some plastic chips into the centre of the table. 'Stay here with me. You're my responsibility.'

'Dad, I'm fifteen.'

'Just let him go, will you?' said one of the men. 'The kid's bored out of his brain. Go ask Robin for a beer. He'll sort you out as long as you don't draw attention to yourself.'

'No beers,' his father said. 'Last thing I need is some

drunk kid on my hands. I spent enough time cleaning up your vomit as a baby.'

'Sure you did,' one of the men said sarcastically. Everyone at the table, except the white-haired man, laughed.

Alyn stepped away from the wall he had been leaning against and went outside. His head was pounding.

Moments later, his father emerged from the door. 'What the hell's the matter with you? Ungrateful little brat. I bring you here to –'

'To watch you play cards all night? Sorry, Dad, but I've got better things to do.'

For a second his father looked like he was going to yell but then his face softened. 'Alyn, I'm sorry,' he said. 'I shouldn't have brought you here. I wasn't thinking. I'm still new to all of this too, you know. It's not been easy.'

Alyn paused. He had a lump in his throat.

'Just give me another chance, will you? I promise I'll make it up to you. We'll do something, just the pair of us.'

Alyn looked at his father – a sinewy, unshaven and pitiful figure pleading with him from the pub doorway.

'Why don't you come back for another game or two?' his father said. 'We'll be finished soon ... I'll even let you play a round.'

'Just get lost, Dad.' Alyn turned and hurried away.

He headed down the road until he found a park. He pushed through the gate, and sat on a bench facing a playground. The swings moved timidly in the breeze.

'Mind if I sit here?'

Alyn looked up. The white-haired man who had been at the card table earlier sat down on the bench beside him.

'Your father got some money out of me tonight,' he chuckled. 'I've never been much good at cards.'

'Neither has my dad. He just got lucky. Who are you anyway – one of his friends or something?'

'No. I'm not. My name is James Felix,' he said, crossing his legs. 'You look like you've had a rough night. I was your age too once –'

'I know what you're going to say – that it's not the end of the world. That I'll look back on it in a few years and laugh.' Alyn gave a disappointed snort. 'That I'm just a teenager who thinks the world revolves round me.'

'Maybe it does . . .'

Alyn looked back at the man suspiciously. 'What are you doing here anyway?'

'The same as you. Thinking.'

'About what?'

'About the difficult decisions we sometimes have to make . . .' Felix trailed off. 'I'm not a bad person, you see.'

'Isn't that what all bad people say?'

'I've not always had money,' Felix explained. 'My parents struggled for most of their lives. My father was a groundskeeper for a very wealthy family. Every year they spent the winter in Italy while he looked after the estate. They had a lot of land, even their own forest with deer. One year when I was eleven or twelve my father took me there to hunt. After about an hour we spotted a deer in among the trees. He handed me the rifle and told me to shoot it. I looked down the scope but I couldn't bring myself to do it. He refused to take the gun from me.

'He said, "If you can't kill an animal yourself, you don't deserve to eat it." That stuck with me.'

'So what happened? Did you shoot it?'

Felix nodded slowly. 'Yes. I shot it. And that's why I'm here, Alyn. I understand what I have to do. You're going to be the first of them, and it's only right that I do this myself.'

'What are you talking about?'

Felix turned to him. 'I could tell you but you probably won't remember anyway.' He removed a cylindrical object from inside his coat. 'I'm sorry, Alyn. I truly am.'

He pointed the metal barrel at Alyn's head and pressed the trigger.

17

Three guards emerged from the blue-tinted mist and marched quickly across the exercise yard towards Alyn.

'They want to see you, Hart,' said the taller of the group, a gaunt man with deep-set eyes who was forever trying to impress Adler.

The warden strode towards him and grabbed Alyn under the arm.

'What are you doing? Let go of me –'

The group marched him swiftly through the snow and they entered the prison through a door on the west side of the building.

Alyn was shoved into a corridor and forcefully manoeuvred up a narrow stairwell. He had never been in this part of the prison before. He could feel his stomach tightening, and had a sense of everything around him falling. *Something isn't right.*

They soon arrived at a door covered in peeling

black paint. 'Go,' one of the group said, pushing him forward in the small of his back.

Alyn turned to the guard. 'Where are we? This isn't Adler's office . . .'

'I never said it was. Go on, go through.' He gave Alyn another shove, relishing the power.

A large floor-to-ceiling window at the far end of the large, featureless room made the teacher appear as little more than a silhouette, while standing to one side by the unpainted wall was Martin Adler. He glared as Alyn approached the table in the centre of the room.

'Prisoner Hart,' the teacher said. 'Please, take a seat.'

'I'd rather stand.'

'As you wish.' She waited until the door was closed and the warden at Alyn's side before sitting down at the table. 'We think you might be better suited to another . . . location.'

'You're moving me?'

'To somewhere a little more *secure*, where your presence won't be as disruptive to the other inmates. You've already had enough second chances, Hart. Your recent antics were the final straw.'

'But I've changed, I swear it. I've given up.' Alyn could feel his voice quivering. '*You've won.*'

'Too late, I'm afraid. You can choose to leave with your dignity, or we can drag you kicking and screaming over the snow for all of your friends to see. The choice is yours.'

Alyn's head was spinning. 'I have friends here,' he said, ashamed of how powerless, how helpless he sounded. 'You can't make me leave them.'

'But you were always so keen to escape,' the teacher said, and drew back with an intake of breath.

'I won't escape again. I promise. I've learned my lesson . . . I've done everything you wanted . . .'

'The wheels are already in motion.' She looked at the guards over Alyn's shoulder. 'Until then I want him kept under the strictest surveillance.'

'Of course,' said Adler, who had moved behind Alyn. 'I'll get two of my best men to escort him.'

'Why are you doing this?' Alyn cried. '*Why are we here?*'

The teacher stood and neatly gathered her files from the table. 'I think our meeting is over, Alyn.'

'You're *sick*,' Alyn hissed. 'All of you, you're sick! How can you stand there and let her do this? There are children in here who haven't seen their parents, their families in months . . . in years . . . How can you let her do this?'

'Quieten down, Hart,' said Adler, who then turned to the teacher. 'Just give the order, and I'll shut him up for you.'

'It's quite all right, Martin. Let him finish.'

'Do none of you even realize what it is you're doing? You've got to know this is wrong!' Alyn's voice was shaking. 'Please, don't let them do this ... There's no reason for it, for any of it –'

'*Everything* we have done is for a reason,' the teacher said, interrupting him. 'Remember that. And one day you might even thank us.'

Before Alyn could stop himself, he had tackled the guard beside him to the wall and was trying to wrestle the ibis from his belt.

Adler and his two men raised their weapons as Alyn and the guard tumbled to the floor, but the guard's body blocked Alyn from their strike.

'For God's sake use your hands for once!' shouted the teacher.

Adler was the first to obey. He rushed towards the pair but, before he could grab hold of Alyn, Alyn had freed the ibis and rolled on to his feet.

A blast whizzed past the guards. Not used to being on the other side of the weapon, Alyn had struggled to find the trigger. He leapt away from an oncoming shot and threw himself over the table.

Papers scattered. Alyn landed on the floor in a tangle as another blast flew overhead and collided against the window. The glass shattered and crashed in a cascade of twinkling shards.

There she is, he thought, noticing the teacher hurrying for the door. *If I could get to her ...*

His fingers tensed round the ibis.

Alyn jumped up, broken glass falling from his hair, and fired again. It was a wayward shot, erratic, but it grazed one of the wardens.

Alyn used the table for cover and aimed for the nearest guard's legs. The blast whizzed out of the baton and struck the man's knee. The guard fell backwards, crashing on to the floor.

The adrenalin was coursing through him now. He clambered to his feet and ran, doubled over, to the far side of the table and crouched.

'Get more back-up!' Adler yelled into the radio. 'I want the stairwell sealed before he can escape –'

Alyn leapt up and fired two ibis blasts in quick succession. Both guards caught the shots in the chest and fell to the floor unconscious. But, before Alyn could celebrate, a pulse roared past the side of his face. He grabbed his ear and winced. Cold air and snow blew in from the now shattered window.

He fired again at Adler, who, despite his size, managed to dodge each of the blasts. Alyn glanced over the table. The tallest guard was closing in on him as he took a breath and sprinted from the cover of a chair, leaping towards the open window.

Alyn turned to fire, striking the guard in the stomach, but the kickback from the ibis threw him off balance. Alyn made an attempt to steady himself but by then it was too late; he was already falling fast out of the window and into the snow.

He landed heavily, the blow sending a painful jolt through his body, but he managed to drag himself to his feet and limp to the large bins that stood along the prison wall, towards the front of the building. The snow had been cleared into the pile that had broken his fall, and his footprints were lost in a swirl of boot marks and muddy tyre tracks.

He waited, wheezing heavily. It wouldn't be long before more guards were sent for. *You won't get a chance like this again.*

Alyn peered round the side of the bins at the guard tower in the distance. Luckily, the lookout seemed to be more concerned with the exercise yard full of teenagers than the side of the prison, which was off-limits.

A truck was parked by the gates. Alyn could see the driver having a cigarette with the security guard in the sentry box nearby. *Making a run for the gate is too predictable*, he thought. Precisely what they would expect.

He noticed there was a green tarpaulin in the back of the truck, covering a couple of crates. Alyn looked back up at the window just in time to see a flurry of movement. It would only be a matter of seconds before the alarm was sounded.

I have to go now, he thought. He moved quietly

round the side of the bins, and limped, half crouching, towards the truck. He pulled himself into the back and slid under the tarpaulin. Then he waited.

'Where do you think Adler is?' said the boy in the cell beside Harlan's. 'It's not like him to be this late.'

'It's Alyn,' Harlan replied, looking through the bars. 'Something's happened to him.'

The doors opened below and Adler and Claude Rayner appeared. Both were tense and panting and covered in flakes of snow.

'What's going on?' someone in the next cell shouted, and the hall was soon a cacophony of questions and murmurs.

Rayner narrowed his eyes. 'Quieten down, everyone!' he boomed, striking his ibis repeatedly against the cell bars.

Ryan watched the unfolding scene with great interest. He spotted an anxious-looking Jes on the other side of the hall.

'*Hey*,' hissed the boy in the cell next to his. 'People are saying Alyn's escaped – for good this time!'

The message was whispered around the prison in a matter of moments, and eventually overheard by Martin Adler on the ground floor.

'I'm sorry to be the bearer of bad news,' he announced, turning back and forth to meet the vista of hopeful, waiting faces. 'But Hart *didn't* escape.'

The chatter instantly fell silent.

'He was captured in the yard after leaping from a window. Broke his leg in the fall.'

'Let's see him then!' someone yelled from the upper level.

'Yeah,' agreed another inmate, roused by the notion of a heroic escape. 'I'm not believing anything until I see it –'

'Then you might be in for a wait; he's already been transferred to another facility. You'll be lucky if you ever see him again.'

Adler had anticipated the inmates' ensuing protests and cut them short.

Jes was the first at the bars of her cell. 'Transferred?' she cried desperately. 'To where? Where have you taken him?'

But her voice was buried under the weight of a hundred others.

18

'You look nice, love,' Jes's mother said as she trotted down the stairs wearing a below-the-knee, long-sleeve dress.

Her father peered at her over his reading glasses. 'Glad to see you dressing sensibly anyway. Where did you say you were going again?'

'Catherine's. We're going to do some revision then watch a film.' Jes smiled sweetly and gave her parents a kiss each. 'I'll be back tomorrow.'

'Don't stay up too late, Jes.' Her father straightened his newspaper. 'You've got exams coming up. I know you think you're immune, but –'

'Oh, let her have just one night of peace,' said her mum, cutting him off. 'You don't realize how lucky we are – Helen's girls go to nightclubs every weekend.'

Jes's father scrutinized her, as though finding her guilty by association. He gave a weary sigh and returned to his newspaper.

Jes flashed her parents a final wave and left the house. Lying on the grass was the plastic bag she'd dropped out of her bedroom window. She scooped it up under her arm and hurried along the path.

Later, almost midnight, the bass from the speakers fluttered through Jes's chest. The air was hard to swallow and the windows were covered with steam from the mass of bodies. Jes tipped back the remains of the bottle and clasped her arms round Catherine and Vicki, dragging them into the crowded living room.

'You know what *we* need?' she shouted to make herself heard over the throbbing drumbeat. 'A holiday! Just the three of us. We'll go after the exams. Let's do it!'

'As if your parents would ever let you go,' Vicki said.

'I'll tell them I'm staying at Cath's,' Jes said, laughing. 'It's worked so far, hasn't it?'

She turned her head to see that an unfamiliar group of boys dripping with gel and aftershave had closed in on them. Dancing, Jes flicked her hair back over her shoulders and smiled at the group. One of the boys watched her, then grinned and moved closer.

'She's not interested,' Catherine said, stepping between them. 'Come on, let's get out of here.'

After managing to divert Jes from the crowded living room and into the hall, Catherine guided her over to the carpeted stairs. 'You all right, Jes? You don't look it.'

'I've got a headache,' Jes said, massaging her temple with her fingertips. She put her empty bottle down.

'You and me both. Sit here. I'll get us both some water.' Catherine weaved round a group of boys by the kitchen door.

I need air, Jes thought, feeling suddenly queasy. She stumbled to the front door and wiped her matted hair away from her eyes. As she walked away from the house, the music echoed in her ears: a muffled thump, fuzzy and whistling.

She was sitting on a wall at the end of the road for a few minutes with her palm across her eyes when a car pulled up alongside her. A window descended.

'Jes Heather?'

'How . . . how do you know my name?' she said in confusion, peeling back the hair from her face.

The door was flung open, and a bald man leapt out, grabbing her round the waist. He dragged her towards the car and threw her in the back seat effortlessly.

'*Help!*' Jes screamed, wriggling and kicking furiously. '*Someone help me! Help me!*'

The man climbed in after her, about to close the door when the point of Jes's heel slammed into his groin. He let out a cry and stumbled backwards, landing on his knees. Jes fumbled with the lock and fell out on to the road on the opposite side of the car, rolling backwards over the gravel.

She kicked off her heels and jumped to her feet before sprinting back towards the house. 'Help! Somebody help me!'

The driver of the car kicked his door open and positioned his ibis across his forearm to steady it. Closing one eye like an archer, he fired and watched as the stunned girl collapsed.

Alyn had been waiting in the back of the truck for what seemed like an age before he heard a rumble of footsteps, driving hard into the snow.

'He must've got over the fence,' he heard Adler say, just inches from where he was hidden. 'Get out there and look for him.' Alyn held his breath. The engine started up and the truck bumped out through the gates.

Curled on his side, he felt every jolt as they rocked across the potted ground. He peered through a gap in the tarpaulin at the desolate white sky and the trees that strained towards it.

About fifteen minutes later the truck came to a halt. Alyn lurched forward, crashing into one of the crates. As one of the truck doors slammed he quietly peeled back the sheet and looked out.

The driver was leaning on a tree with one arm,

talking into his radio. 'There's no sign of him on the road. I've gone for miles. He wouldn't have made it this far on foot.'

There was a reply from the other end that Alyn couldn't make out.

'Of course I won't mention it. Tell Rayner there must be footprints coming off the road somewhere. If he's escaped then he's in the forest, and good luck to him in this weather.'

Alyn looked at the forest with a growing sense of alarm. The guard was right. It would soon be night and his thin uniform and outdoor coat were not enough to keep him warm. He'd have to hope that some form of shelter lay out there in the wilderness.

Without further hesitation, Alyn crept to his feet and hopped down into the snow. Not knowing which direction he was heading, or where he was going, he ran.

'There you are,' the teacher said, placing a hand on Jes's shoulder. 'Come inside. I want to speak with you in private.'

Jes went into the classroom. The teacher gestured for her to sit at a desk near the front.

'I'm not in trouble, am I?'

'Not yet. Unless there's something you want to tell me?'

'No, Miss. Nothing.'

The teacher smiled. 'I thought we'd talk. I'd like to know how you've been getting on since our last meeting.'

'Fine,' Jes said. 'I'm getting on fine.'

'No more *delusions*?'

'Delusions?'

'Of your alleged innocence. You were always one of our more troublesome inmates.'

'I've changed.' Jes spoke softly, trying to evoke the distant, passive tone of the turned prisoners. 'I'm learning to accept what I've done. I'm guilty. I know that now. *We're all guilty.*'

The teacher crossed her legs. Deep in thought, she clicked the end of her fountain pen rhythmically.

'I hope you're not just saying that to impress me.'

Of course I am. I've seen what happens to the ones who try to fight it.

'Of course not.'

The teacher placed the pen on the table, then moved it with her finger, making sure it lay dead centre. 'And has there been any temptation for you to steal?'

Jes hesitated. *This could be a trap.*

'Would you like me to repeat the question?'

'There is always temptation,' she blurted out. '*Always.*' She lowered her eyes. 'But I'm trying.'

'You were close with Alyn, weren't you?'

'We were friends.'

'Just friends?' The teacher let her blush, then said,

'I don't expect you to answer that. Did you have any idea that he was going to try to escape again?'

'No.'

'He said nothing of it to you, even though you were . . . "friends"?'

'No. Because otherwise I would have said goodbye.' Jes swallowed. 'I didn't have the chance.'

'Not that it is even important now, but did he ever tell you his plans for when he made it over the fence?'

Jes shook her head.

'He had no plans? And no strategy whatsoever? Is that what you're telling me, Jes?'

'If he did, he wouldn't share them with me. It's hard to have a strategy when you don't even know where you are.' Jes looked up. 'Please,' she insisted, 'you have to tell me he's OK.'

'I'll do no such thing,' came the reply. 'The prison will be a far better place without Hart and his dangerous fantasies. If I find out you're lying, about any of this, your punishment will be severe. But for now I'm finished with you. Get back to your cell, Miss Heather.'

'Thank you,' Jes replied. She shuffled the chair away from the desk and quickly left the room.

19

After her interrogation, Jes found Ryan in the yard, kicking a football around with some of the others. The wind was accelerating, scattering a light snowfall across the prison.

An eighteen-year-old Scottish boy, who had been brought in just a couple of weeks after her, was struggling to manoeuvre the scuffed leather ball round clumps of hard snow. 'The hoop,' he said, and pointed to a wilted basketball hoop hanging several feet above the goalposts. He chipped the ball and watched as it sailed through the air. 'It's in!'

One of the boys laughed as it smashed through, sending the hoop rattling and trembling violently. The ball then hit a mound of snow and bounced some way across the yard.

Ryan looked impressed. 'Didn't know you were that good.'

'Neither did I.'

As Ryan turned round, he spotted Jes sitting on a

bench by the fence. 'I'm sure Alyn will be all right, whatever happened,' he said as he shuffled in beside her. 'Don't dwell on it.'

'Easier said than done.'

'I know it's hard but you have to stay focused, Jes. I don't want you to lose your drive. One way or another, I'm getting out of here. There's no going back. Are you in?'

'I'm in.'

'Good.' He smiled, then nodded to Elsa, who was standing nearby listening, the hood of her outdoor coat flapping in the wind. 'It looks like our team is coming together after all.'

'So what do you think?' Elsa said, coming closer and distractedly kicking a hard lump of snow at the fence.

'About?'

'Alyn, of course.' Elsa swung her leg at another lump and watched it hit the wire and crumble into powder.

'Who knows what to believe in this place,' Ryan said. 'They can't open their mouths without lying.'

'If there's even the slightest chance he's escaped, he'll tell everyone. They'll send the police and we'll be free in no time,' Elsa said.

'We're not sitting back and waiting for it to happen,' said Jes. 'We want you to join us.'

'Join you? For what?'

'What do you think?'

'Oh.' Elsa's eyes widened.

Jes looked around the yard, making sure they weren't being watched. 'You're one of the few people I trust, Elsa. And I know you want to get out of here as much as we do.'

'They already threatened me with solitary. I don't know what I'd do if they put me in there . . .'

Jes looked disappointed. 'You already think we're going to fail.'

'It's a risk. A complete gamble – what makes you think we're going to pull it off?'

'The *tunnel*,' said Ryan.

Elsa turned to him and scoffed. 'The tunnel that might not even exist and could be anywhere? We've been looking for months. I think even Harlan's close to giving up.'

'I think our search might be over,' said Ryan.

'I don't follow . . .'

Jes leant in close to Elsa. 'One of the reasons Harlan is even digging that tunnel is to get into the ventilation system – because of a vent he saw in *the guards' room*. The guards thought you were looking for a vent . . . in the *cupboard*. Two vents – it's safe to assume the two are connected, right? If one of us could get inside the vent in the cupboard, we could crawl through it to the guards' room.'

'Why would we want to do that?'

'You know what they keep in there? *Plans*. The prison blueprints are in a cabinet beneath the window,' said Jes.

'How do you know that?'

'Alyn. He saw them in there a few months ago while he was being interrogated by Adler. Once we find the blueprints, we find the tunnel. But we need someone else: someone small enough to crawl through the vent,' she added more pointedly.

Elsa mulled it over. 'I don't know. It just seems too dangerous. Do you not have a back-up plan . . .'

'This *is* the back-up plan,' said Ryan.

'We don't have long, Elsa.' Jes looked at her pleadingly.

Wearily, Elsa turned to stare at the prison. A snowflake fluttered on to her nose.

'All right,' she said, and almost immediately felt her stomach sink. 'I'm in.'

The truck slowed by the gates, crackling and crunching over lumps of slick, hard ice.

The young man posted in the sentry box lifted the window and peered out, shielding his eyes from the flurry of falling snow. 'Any luck finding him?'

The driver shook his head. 'But you keep that to yourself. As far as everyone here is concerned, he's been transferred. Last thing we want is the rest of them getting any ideas.'

The man in the sentry box nodded and raised the gate. As the truck inched forward, the driver flashed a wave to the group of guards, led by Claude Rayner, who were trudging towards the forest.

I'd hate to be in the boy's shoes, he thought, trying his best to avoid Rayner's eyes.

20

One year ago

'So what do you think?' asked Felix.

The disused factory – or prison as it was soon to be – peered back at them from behind the trees. The Prime Minister shivered, unable to shake a feeling of despair. 'I suppose it will have to do. Though I find it all rather eerie.'

'You should see it when it snows. It looks beautiful.'

I can't imagine this ever looking beautiful, the Prime Minister thought, squinting at the mass of stained grey concrete, but decided to give Felix the benefit of the doubt. 'I just don't see why they have to be children,' he said. 'Is there no other way?'

'As I already explained, the effect seems to be far more potent with them. Perhaps as we grow older we learn to stop it from happening. And, of course, they're easier to break.'

'How long, do you think?'

'We think a couple of years will be enough to give things a push in the right direction.'

'And you're quite sure it will work? That you will be able to restore some . . . order . . . ? That we will be able to regain control?'

'I'm certain,' came a voice from behind the pair. They both turned to find a woman in her mid-forties approaching with an extended hand.

'Prime Minister,' said Felix. 'I would like you to meet Susannah Dion. She will be overseeing the facility.'

The Prime Minister warily took Susannah's hand. 'I assume you're part of this *Pledge*, are you, Ms Dion?'

'Not quite. I'm a psychologist, among other things, although the children will know me as their teacher. Mr Felix caught wind of what I was doing some years ago and was kind enough to fund my research.'

'You mean you discovered the –'

'The strategy? As much as I'd like to, I can't take *all* the credit.' Susannah paused. 'Something is troubling you, Prime Minister?'

'I've always considered myself a rational man, Ms Dion. This is all just . . . very new to me. I'm still trying to get my head around everything. The logistics of the situation.'

'I can assure you that once the project is under way, any doubts you have will cease. But, in the meantime, I have something that might reassure you.' Susannah handed a wad of paper to the Prime Minister.

'What is this?'

'Proof. That we aren't wasting our time.'

The Prime Minister riffled through the papers with his thumb. 'This means nothing to me. It's just pages and pages of numbers . . .'

'Look closer.'

He reluctantly opened the document to a page near the middle.

'Notice anything?'

'The numbers seem to be random. Until here.' He pointed at a string where the number eight was repeated thirty-two times in a row.

Susannah smiled. 'Quite wonderful, isn't it? As thrilling as any novel, as sublime as poetry.'

'You and I obviously have very different tastes in art, Ms Dion.'

'Turn to the next page, and look about halfway down.'

The Prime Minister sighed, and did as she asked. This time, amid the jumble of random numbers, the number eight was repeated again for several lines.

'A random number generator,' she explained. 'Influenced by extraordinary means. It's true what they say – number really is the last refuge of magic.'

She accepted the folder back from the Prime Minister. 'What you saw was just one child. Imagine what you might see with five, ten, fifty . . . *one hundred* – a significant number.'

The Prime Minister was about to speak when the sound of a rattling engine interrupted his train of thought. He looked past the psychologist, watching as a truck crawled over the uneven ground and disappeared behind the trees.

'Those are our first residents,' Susannah said. 'Right on time. If you'll both excuse me for a moment.'

Felix and the Prime Minister nodded as Susannah left them and meandered through the trees towards the prison gates.

'She certainly seems eager to get this under way.'

'As are we all,' said Felix. 'Things are going to change, Prime Minister. For the better.'

'So you keep telling me. I will hold you to your word, Felix. These past twelve months have been difficult to say the least.' He paused, looking deep in thought. 'Tell me, does it ever concern you that you might be playing God?'

Felix looked at the heavy clouds. 'Someone has to,' he said sadly, brushing away a branch.

'This project wouldn't have any other hidden benefits I might not be aware of, would it?'

'I'm not sure I understand . . .'

'If the country is on the brink of a collapse there would be repercussions for everyone. Including yourselves.'

'Our aim is to serve the country, Prime Minister. I thought I had made myself clear.'

The Prime Minister forced a smile and started to walk away, but then turned back to Felix and said, 'You said something to me that night you and I met. It's been playing on my mind ever since. You told me there was someone else involved in this Pledge?'

'Yes, my adviser. I recall telling you back then that he wasn't one for publicity.'

'Even now?'

Felix smiled. 'A secret society has to have *some* secrets, doesn't it?'

In the distance, through the trees, were the sounds of their prisoners being pulled from the truck.

'I suppose it does,' the Prime Minister conceded.

He looked at the prison a final time then pulled the hood of his raincoat down across his eyes, as if to shield himself from the truth of what he had agreed. He trampled quickly over the fallen leaves, to the waiting helicopter, trying his best to block out the screams and cries.

21

While Jes and Ryan were busy recruiting, Julian ambled slowly around the exercise yard by himself. A freezing damp wind tore wildly at his hair.

He came to rest by the fence and let his eyes drift to the game of football taking place. 'A remarkable waste of time,' Julian muttered, considering the absurdity of the game and the ferocious enthusiasm with which it was played. Maybe if they invited him to join in he might enjoy it. But there was no chance of that.

At that moment the ball came hurtling towards him and, before he could move out of the way, it crashed into his leg. Julian winced. A ball striking his shin on a cold day was a poignant – and painful – reminder of his school days. More often than not it had been deliberate.

'*Oi! Pass it back!*' someone from the pitch yelled. Julian drew his leg back and swung.

The ball flew wide of its intended target. A couple

of boys jeered. *Absurd game*, he concluded, and hastily soothed his stinging leg with his fingers.

Julian looked down to where the ball had landed and noticed something half buried in the snow: a shiny sliver of black metal.

He glanced over at the guards, who were huddled by the door, then lowered himself slowly to his knees.

'An ibis?' He exhaled, frantically patting away the snow.

When he was sure that no one was watching, he shoved the weapon inside his coat and cradled it under his arm.

'Look out!' came a cry from the yard. Julian glanced up to see the ball speeding towards him a second time. He ducked, but the ball clipped the back of his head. Julian teetered on the ice, trying to stabilize himself. His legs shot out from under him.

Julian reclaimed the ibis just as a miserable-looking Adler stamped towards him through the snow.

'Sleave,' Adler said. 'I hear you made quite an impression with the others in my absence.'

'I'm ... delighted.' Julian pulled his coat tighter, and struggled to get to his feet.

'Don't be; it wasn't a good one. You look pale. Not sleeping?'

Julian shook his head, then contradicted himself with a quick nod. 'I'm sleeping fine.'

Adler took a step closer. 'I don't think I ever got

the chance to tell you how much I appreciated the tip-off.'

'Oh?'

Adler smiled and nodded.

What was he after? Julian could feel the ibis slipping from his grasp under the coat.

'If I hadn't put an extra man in the corridor, we might have had some problems.'

Julian gave an anaemic smile.

Adler watched the playing inmates with some suspicion and moved his mouth closer to Julian's ear. 'Haven't heard anything else recently, have you, Sleave?' he said.

'No. Not a thing.'

'That's odd. Because I recall Claude telling me you had some information you wanted to share.'

'Oh that? I thought I overheard something in the canteen. Rumours of an escape. It was nothing.'

Adler drew closer. 'You know, withholding information isn't a wise idea. All it takes is a single word from my lips and you'll find all those privileges you've worked so hard for disappearing. You've had it easy up till now. How about I have you sharing with one of those idiots on the ground floor? Or even Farrell? Because I could, Sleave. Just like that.' Adler clicked his fingers; his thick gloves softened the snap.

'If anything comes to me you'll be the first person

I tell.' Julian could feel the ibis slipping further inside his coat. 'I – I'm not feeling too good. I'm going inside for a little while.'

Julian went hurrying across the snow and when he was out of Adler's sight he pulled the ibis back up under his arm. *Things just got a lot more interesting,* he thought.

'Any luck?' Jes asked as Ryan approached her. His hood was up, and his ears were pink with cold.

He shook his head. 'Seems like everyone was just waiting for Alyn to bust them out ... Either that or they don't trust me enough to tell me. What about you?'

'Do I trust you?' Jes asked facetiously.

'I meant the recruiting.'

'Well, it's not exactly like we have people queuing up.'

'Actually you do,' said Harlan, who had been listening to the pair's conversation. 'I want in – although like the pair of you it's *out* I really want.'

Ryan looked at Jes. 'What do you say?'

She nodded. 'We can trust Harlan. You're still digging, right? Do you really think you'll find that tunnel?'

'I don't know whether or not we'll find it. But we have to go through that wall and see what's inside. There's a cavity of some sort.'

'If you're not careful you'll dig right into Julian's cell. If he finds out we're planning something . . .'

'He won't.' At that moment the bell rang. 'We'll speak about this later,' Harlan said, as the guards began shepherding them back inside.

22

Julian waited until evening before removing the ibis from underneath his mattress. The weapon was a lot lighter than he had imagined. He ran his fingers over the cool metal, twirling it between his hands and letting his thumb rest upon the trigger. The temptation to let a bolt of sound burst through the bars of his cell was almost overwhelming. With some reluctance Julian lifted his thumb from the trigger.

He crawled underneath the bed and removed a brick from the wall. He had managed to free it after months of chipping away at the cement with a screwdriver he'd stolen from one of the guards.

Inside the wall Julian had amassed a small collection of trinkets and things that might one day prove useful: a fork, a ball, a watch. Even a battered copy of *The Tempest* from the guards' room.

Julian often lay awake for hours at night, intoxicating himself with all manner of daring and outlandish fantasies of how he might escape. The ball, if placed at the correct point under the armpit, would hinder the flow of blood to the arm and could create the illusion of a stopped pulse – an old magician's trick, but a surprisingly effective one that just might get him admitted to the sick room. The fork could potentially be a lethal weapon, especially if all but one of the prongs were flattened. Once he was free the watch could be pawned for money, which could provide him with food and shelter.

He carefully slipped the ibis inside the cavity and returned the brick to its place. He would need to act soon, but for now he would sleep on it.

'Here,' said Harlan as he tossed a couple of clean uniforms into a locked cell earlier that evening. He pushed the squeaking trolley to the next, gathered a folded uniform for Ryan and launched it through the bars.

'Now everyone's agreed, we need to arrange a meeting,' Ryan said to Harlan in a lowered voice. 'Think we can use your cell at recess tomorrow?'

'Sure.'

'And there's something else I want to ask you. Something you said in the yard the other day. About me feeling *different*.'

'Has it been happening to you too? The coincidences, I mean ... the patterns ...'

Before Ryan could reply he noticed they were being

watched by a thin, sickly-looking boy with hair so pale it seemed white.

'What are you looking at?' Ryan snarled at him.

The boy gazed at Ryan with a passivity that verged on sadness, and quietly left.

'That's not the first time I've seen him snooping around us. Who is he?'

'His name's Tom,' Harlan replied, returning to the trolley and ready to move on. 'He used to be on our side. He always swore they'd never turn him. But they did. He's gone a little – how can I say this? – *evangelical*.'

Harlan looked at Ryan sombrely and moved on to the next cell, where a boy lay asleep.

We have to get out of here soon, Ryan thought, drumming his fingers anxiously on the wall.

While Harlan was handing out uniforms, Jes took a diversion to the store cupboard on the way to her chores. She peered at the upper shelves, looking for evidence of the vent she had overheard the guards discussing.

After finding no sign of it, she lowered herself to a crouch, pulling aside a couple of storage boxes. Reaching behind, Jes's fingers brushed against a sliver of metal.

'Got it,' she exhaled, revealing the grated vent.

Jes gave it a tug but the grate was tightly screwed. Unfortunately, there was only one person she knew with a screwdriver.

23

Rayner lowered himself to one knee and gestured to his two colleagues to freeze.

He peered through the trees, each breath a slow, deep rattle in his lungs. Was there even something there? The landscape played all manner of tricks on the eyes and the blazing whiteness caused Rayner to squint. 'Someone's up there,' he whispered, wiping his forearm across his grey stubble.

'I can't see anything,' said the guard beside him, craning his neck forward. 'Are you sure, boss?'

Rayner said nothing as a peal of thunder rumbled overhead.

'We should head back,' said a red-headed man who was a little way behind them. 'If we get caught in a storm, we –'

'He'll be caught in it too,' Rayner cut in. 'It might be just what we need to flush him out . . .'

'This is no use,' complained the first guard. 'I'm heading back to the prison.'

Before he could turn, Rayner grabbed him and slammed him against a tree with such force the man wheezed. 'You just don't get it, do you?'

'Look, Claude, I –'

Rayner tightened his grip on the guard's coat. His fingers were numbed and blue in the cold.

'He's a criminal. A violent, dangerous criminal and you're happy to see him roaming the streets?'

'That's not what I meant –'

'What about the next death he causes? You want blood on your hands? You think you could live with that?'

'N-no . . . of course not, boss.'

Rayner reluctantly released him and turned to the other two men. 'Unless you – unless all of you – want to lose your jobs, I suggest you start looking for him. Is that understood?'

'Yes, sir,' they replied.

Sleet began to spit at them through the quivering branches, but they traipsed on regardless, all too aware of the consequences of disobeying orders.

After an hour of walking they were all shivering violently, and their clothes were wet and stiff. Darkness was beginning to settle and the group converged briefly to light a fire.

Rayner leant down and nestled his palms over his eyes. His head was throbbing.

'What if he's dead, boss?' said the red-headed

guard, digging in his bag for food. 'I mean, he could already be buried under all this snow. We could be sitting on him right now.'

It was a fair point, not one Rayner had even considered. In his mind's eye it was him who was responsible for bringing the boy back to the prison by the scruff of the neck.

'No. He's still here,' Rayner muttered and bit down hard into a sandwich. His jaws cracked as he chewed. 'He may have gone further than we thought but he's still out here.'

Rayner eventually tossed the remains of the sandwich into the snow and got up, brushing crumbs from his hands. Out of the corner of his eye he noticed something: a track, a single boot print, preserved in the shade of a tree.

'Over here,' he called to the others. 'I've found something.'

The guards obediently dropped their food and raced over.

'It's fresh,' Rayner said. 'Probably not much older than an hour or so.'

'Is it Hart's?'

Rayner scratched his stubble. 'No,' he said after a couple of moments. 'No.'

'No?'

'Look,' Rayner said. 'The print. It's not standard uniform.'

The other guards leant closer.

'There's someone else here,' Rayner said.

'You think someone might've discovered the prison?'

'It's miles from anywhere. And the land is private property,' another guard said.

'That doesn't usually stop people.'

Before Rayner could intervene his radio hissed through the fabric of his coat. '*Claude, it's Martin. What did you find?*'

'A track,' said Rayner, brushing his hair back from his brow. 'But it doesn't belong to Hart.'

A single slow breath crackled through the radio, but, other than that, Adler was unnervingly silent.

'I'm going to take some men first thing in the morning,' Rayner continued. 'We'll set up camp out there and see what we can find. With your permission, of course.'

The guards shared a disappointed look behind Rayner's back.

'*Permission granted. I'll see you back at the prison.*'

'Better prepare your sleeping bags, boys,' Rayner said, and shoved the radio back inside his pocket. 'We're going camping.'

24

'You can sit down,' the teacher said, watching the inmates file into the classroom after breakfast the following morning.

When they were all seated she made them affirm their guilt, watching the moving mouths and lowered eyes with a steely intensity.

'Good,' she said, once they'd finished the recital. 'I'm glad we don't have any problems today.'

She was about to take her seat when she noticed Ryan sitting towards the back with his arms folded. 'Farrell,' she said. 'Why don't you come to the front?'

Ryan cautiously left his seat and shuffled between the rows of desks, feeling every pair of eyes burning into him.

'I'm sure you know Mr Farrell by now,' she announced to the class, then turned to Ryan. 'Mr Farrell believes he is innocent. That he hasn't done anything wrong. Do you agree with that?'

'No,' they said.

'I've changed my mind, Miss,' he cut in. 'I know I did wrong. I know I'm guilty. I've accepted all of that . . .'

He noticed Jes, who seemed to exhale with relief at his confession.

'You're a liar, Farrell. I can see you're trouble,' the teacher said. 'I can see you haven't changed a bit.'

'I swear it, I –'

'Guards, I want you to put him in that chair. Hold his hand on the table.'

Before Ryan could respond, he found himself shoved into the chair. One of the men grabbed his right arm and held it, palm up, against the table. 'What are you doing?' he protested. 'Let go of me . . .'

The teacher beckoned to Jes. 'You can come here too.'

Jes obediently stood and walked over to the table. Her expression was downcast, feigning the servility of the other inmates.

'I am very proud of what Miss Heather has achieved.' She put an arm on Jes's shoulder. 'She has managed to overcome many of the delusions and fantasies that held her back for so long. She has learned to accept.' She gestured for Jes to sit at the table opposite Ryan. 'Perhaps you will be better at influencing him.'

'I don't think he needs influencing,' Jes murmured, watching Ryan. 'I think he's sorry. I think he wants to change.'

'Come now, don't be so naive.' The teacher removed a small wad of pristine, shiny paper from the table beneath the projector screen and pushed it towards Jes.

'What do I do?'

'You help him change his mind. You tell him to say he's innocent.'

Jes turned her eyes to Ryan. 'Say you're innocent.'

'I'm . . . I'm innocent,' Ryan answered, confused.

'Now cut him.'

'What?'

The teacher snatched the paper from Jes's hand and drew it quickly across Ryan's knuckles.

He inhaled, wincing. A faint red slit appeared in his skin.

'You'll be surprised how quickly someone can learn. You were a fast learner. All it takes is the right teacher.' She handed the paper back to Jes. 'Now you continue.'

'I don't want to hurt him.'

The teacher looked at her with mounting suspicion. 'If you're unable to do it, I may be forced to reconsider your progress . . .'

'I'm – I'm trying to be a better person,' Jes pleaded. 'How can I be a better person if I hurt someone?'

'This is your last chance. Ask him to say he's innocent.'

Do it, Ryan urged silently. *You need to play along . . .*

'If you don't do it, I will. Now ask him to say –'

'*You're innocent*,' Jes interrupted, staring deep into Ryan's eyes. 'Say you're innocent.'

'I'm innocent,' Ryan said quietly. Trembling, Jes picked up the paper and swept it across his hand.

I'm sorry, Jes wanted to say, watching him grimace.

'Good.' The teacher smiled. 'Now continue. I'll tell you when I think he's had enough.'

'Say . . . say you're innocent,' Jes said barely above a whisper.

Ryan answered breathily and she positioned the paper edge over his clammy index finger and snatched it away.

'I'm innocent,' he repeated.

After what seemed like an age, Ryan's hand was damp with sweat and covered in a maze of unclosed wounds that stung each time the air shifted.

'Enough,' said the teacher. The guards released Ryan and marched back to the doors. Clutching his wrist, Ryan slumped back to his desk.

'Thank you,' the teacher said to Jes. 'It seems that you have far more influence over him than I do.'

'You're welcome,' Jes said bitterly. The projector had already started rolling by the time she returned to her desk.

She sat on her hands to try to keep them from trembling and looked over at Ryan, who was hunched over with his red hand palm down on the table.

Trying to put his punishment out of her mind, Jes raised her eyes to the screen just in time to catch the flicker of a spliced frame.

There it is again, she thought, desperately trying to discern the picture. Out of the corner of her eye, she noticed Julian, his head tilted slightly to one side. He mouthed something at her but Jes quickly looked away and sat through the rest of the film, forcing herself not to blink. The distorted soundtrack and rigid authoritarian narration washed over her.

Almost fifteen minutes passed and Jes's eyes were burning. It was then that the image appeared a final time and all became clear. It was a technical drawing of an electronic device attached by a bundle of wires to a digital timer and two blocks of explosives.

A bomb.

25

'How's the hand?' Jes said, smiling sympathetically at Ryan in the canteen later that day.

He tried to smile back. 'It's all right. Didn't hurt that much. I got bored after the first few minutes.'

'Don't lie. I could see you flinching across the table.' Jes lifted his wrist and examined the papercuts on his hand. 'I'm sorry.'

'It wasn't your fault. It's not like you wanted to do it. What kind of maniac would make you do that?'

'She's a sadist.'

'She's crazy. And what was that lesson about? Showing us those weird old videos . . .'

Jes was about to share her discovery when she noticed Julian had just settled into a seat. 'I've got to go,' she said. 'And I'm sorry. Again.'

Ryan nodded and walked away, holding his hand protectively.

Julian eyed Jes as she neared his table. 'What do you want?'

'A favour.'

'Go on.'

'I need something,' she said in a hushed voice as she sat down. 'Something I know you've got . . .'

'Cunning? Intelligence?'

'A screwdriver.'

Julian made eyes at her then looked away. 'I don't know what you're talking about.'

'Come on, Julian – I saw you steal it that time. And I didn't say anything to the guards.'

Julian smiled, enjoying her frustration. 'Why do you need a screwdriver?'

'Forget it,' she huffed. 'It doesn't matter.' She went to stand up but Julian stopped her.

'I might be able to help. But first I'll need to know why.'

It took Jes some moments to gather the courage to say it. 'We want out.'

'I figured as much. Why now?'

'Look around.'

Julian glanced up. There seemed to be an endless array of blank faces, each in identical grey boiler suits. He looked at the defeated expressions and the distant eyes, and felt his skin prickle.

'How long is it going to be before they break us too?' Jes said. 'I don't know how much longer I can go on. That's why I need the screwdriver, Julian. So we can get out of here.'

Julian hesitated. 'I'll think about it.' He stood up from his seat. 'I've seen them too,' he said, in parting. 'The spliced frames in the films. They're subliminal messages.'

'They're what?'

Julian looked weary. 'Advertisers used to sneak them into films to try to make you buy their products. They probably still do for all I know but that may just be the cynic in me talking. They're flashed up so quickly that you aren't supposed to see them. Consciously anyway. Brainwashing is probably too strong a term. It's more . . . *suggestive*.'

'And why are they trying to suggest *bombs*? Are they trying to get us to blow something up?'

Julian shrugged. 'That, Jes,' he considered languidly, 'is a very good question.'

'Julian?' said Ryan, as the group were stood together in a corner of the yard, a short while later. 'You mean the one nobody trusts? No way. What were you thinking?'

'If we don't get that screwdriver, we don't get in the vent. If we don't get in the vent we don't find the plans, and we don't find the tunnel – and we don't get out of here.'

'There has to be another way. A way that doesn't involve *him*.' He nodded towards Julian, who was now talking with one of the guards. 'He's probably repeating everything you said . . .'

'I didn't tell him anything.'

Elsa frowned. 'Why don't we just tell the guards that he's got a stash somewhere in his room. I'm sure they'll find it if they look hard enough.'

'I'm with Elsa,' said Ryan. 'I say we give him a taste of his own medicine . . .'

Jes shook her head. 'That stash is much more useful to us if Julian has it. If the guards find it, it won't be of use to anyone.'

Ryan looked up and caught sight of Tom watching them. 'We need to be more careful,' he hissed, gesturing towards the white-haired boy with his eyes.

'Careful of what?' asked Jes. 'It's not like we've made any real progress. We need to sit down and start putting things into motion. No more waiting.'

26

'Excuse me, Mr Felix?'

James Felix had just left his company's offices in Canary Wharf when he heard his name called. He turned to find himself face to face with a woman in her early thirties, although with her tired eyes and unwashed hair she could have easily passed for much older at first glance.

'My name's Laura Farrell.'

'I'm afraid that means nothing to me.'

'I work for you,' she added.

'You do? I don't recall ever seeing you . . .'

'I'm a cleaner,' she said, and removed an identification card from her coat pocket. 'I work in your factory up in Sheffield.'

Felix took the card and nodded before handing it back to her.

'I've come to ask for your help, Mr Felix. I don't know where else to go –'

'My help?' Felix dismissed her with a flick of his

hand. 'I'm awfully sorry, Ms Farrell, but I'm not a charity . . .'

'No,' she urged. 'Mr Felix, there must be something you can do –'

'If you've lost your job, there's really very little I can do apart from offer you some consolation in the fact that you're not alone. If you'd like to apply for something else –'

'It's not my job.'

Already her voice was beginning to break. She looked away. 'It's my son. He's only sixteen. A boy. He – he's missing.'

'Missing?' Felix took an embroidered silk handkerchief from his pocket and handed it to her.

She nodded, blowing her nose. 'He'd never run away, Mr Felix. His dad left us when he was only little. He'd never leave me. He promised he'd always look after me . . .'

'I assume you've spoken to the police?'

The woman nodded again.

'Miss Farrell, I am terribly sorry to hear this. But I don't understand what I could possibly do to help . . .'

'You're the wealthiest man in the country,' she said, taking a step towards him. 'You must be able to help; you could set up a reward or something. You could . . .'

Felix considered this for a moment and rubbed his temple. 'What did you say your son's name was?'

'His name is Ryan. Ryan Farrell.'

'Ryan Farrell,' Felix pondered, until it dawned on him where he recognized the name from. *He's one of ours.*

'I-I'm sorry, Miss Farrell. But I'm afraid there's really nothing I can do . . .' Felix gave what he hoped was a sympathetic smile and hurried away, gripping his briefcase tightly.

When he was some way along the street, out of the woman's sight, he felt his phone vibrating in his pocket. 'Susannah,' he hissed. 'I thought we agreed that you would never call me unless –'

'Yes, unless there was an emergency,' she interrupted. 'I don't quite know how to break this to you, James, but we have a problem . . . One of the prisoners has escaped.'

27

Alyn staggered along on legs that no longer felt as though they belonged to him. Barely able to see a thing in the dark, he lurched from one tree to the next, grabbing, grasping. His breath released in a hoarse whisper from his lips, and each pull of air felt like he was sucking ice into his lungs.

Keep moving, he told himself. *You can't stop. You'll die. It has to end soon. It has to end.*

He felt himself growing confused and disorientated at the sound of the harsh wind singing into his ears, and the memories and thoughts from earlier that he had not yet had the chance to subdue with sleep seemed to be repeating and replaying, as heavy and clumsy as his body.

'If you stop, you'll die,' he said aloud, and it sounded like the voice wasn't his. '*Keep moving.*'

28

Rayner and his team of three guards hitched a ride on the delivery truck the morning after Alyn's escape. They drove about ten miles from the prison; the ground was a grey slushy mix of tyre tracks, mud and crusts of dirty snow. Rayner took a long breath, sucking in the scent of wet leaves.

'Where to, boss?' yawned one of the men, slipping his arms under the straps of his backpack. His eyes were red and puffy and a light growth of stubble covered his neck and jaw.

Rayner made a sweeping gesture with his hand. 'There's no way he could've got further than this in the dark. He's probably been going round in circles. We should start here and work our way back.'

They set off into the trees, brushing away overhanging branches.

'We'll get more ground covered if we split into two groups.' Rayner pointed into the forest. 'And if you see or hear *anything*, you radio me immediately.'

'Yes, boss.'

The third guard tugged a woolly hat down over his ears and followed after Rayner, who was holding his ibis tightly. The pair marched in silence for almost an hour.

'We're going to have some trouble bringing him in,' Rayner eventually said. 'You know how dangerous they are. I've never heard Martin so insistent, and I've known him for more years than you've probably been alive . . .'

'Maybe he knows something we don't.' The guard adjusted his rucksack. The straps were starting to chafe his shoulders.

'You know,' Rayner said, 'there's always a chance we might not bring him in alive.'

'Sir?'

Rayner studied his companion for a few moments, then smiled. 'Just a thought.'

Out of the corner of his eye, the guard saw a figure, barely a shadow, passing between the trees, several metres away. 'Did you see that?'

'Yes,' Rayner whispered.

The guard noticed his boss's ibis was trembling slightly.

'Stay low.'

They crept to the treeline through the creaking snow, trying to step as lightly as possible.

'Go to the right,' Rayner instructed. 'I'll go straight ahead. We'll trap him.'

He gripped the ibis in both hands and ducked under a branch. A light sprinkling of snow tumbled on to his head.

'I think we've lost him,' the guard hissed through the trees.

He was immediately silenced by Rayner who pressed a gloved finger to his lips.

Rayner sprinted forward and shot two, three times. The figure ducked, and then disappeared behind a tree.

'We've got him. He's surrounded.' Rayner fired again but the blast whizzed into the snow.

'*Come out, Hart!*' Rayner could feel his heart pounding hard through his coat.

'This is your last warning. Step out with your hands behind your head . . .'

From out of the trees came a man. He was slim and sinewy, in his early sixties, with a scraggly white beard. He wore several layers of clothing, the outermost layer being a heavy, tattered overcoat.

'Who are you?' asked Rayner.

'My – my name's Henry,' the stranger panted, looking back and forth between the two men.

'That means nothing to me. Now, tell me again, who are you? What are you doing here?'

'I was hiking. I entered the forest by the motorway.

I thought I knew where I was going but . . .' He trailed off, looking embarrassed. 'I got lost.'

Rayner made eyes at his colleague. 'Why did you run?'

'Because you were firing at me. I'd say that's as good a reason as any. What are those things you're holding? They look like –'

'They're tasers,' the guard lied. 'You are aware that this is private property?'

'Private property? I didn't see any signs . . .'

It was true enough. There were no signs whatsoever; after all, signs would only have drawn unwanted attention.

'Why are you carrying tasers?'

'We're looking for someone,' Rayner told him. 'A boy. You haven't happened to see a boy in these woods, have you?'

'A *boy*? Out here?'

'Just answer the question.'

'I haven't seen any boy. In fact, I haven't seen anyone here but you two. Come to think of it, I've barely seen a bird. So who is this boy anyway, and why are you looking for him? He's not in some kind of trouble, is he?'

'The exit is that way,' Rayner growled, pointing north. 'If you keep walking, you'll find the road soon enough.'

Henry nodded. 'Thank you. And good day to the pair of you. I hope you find your boy.'

The pair watched him walk away through the trees, until all that was left of him was a trail of crumbling boot prints in the snow.

29

During the final recess for that day, Elsa acted as lookout while the others sat in a circle on the floor of Harlan's cell. Ryan laid out the sketches he had made of the floor plan on the paper towels.

'Here's the cupboard,' he said, pointing to his map. 'And this is the guards' room.'

Jes looked over at Elsa. 'The room is locked during chores. If we could find some way of distracting them while you went inside . . .'

'Why does it have to be me?'

''Cause you're the only one who'll fit, that's why,' Ryan said. He turned to Harlan. 'How's the digging coming along?'

'Slowly. The boy in the next cell was awake for most of the night, so I couldn't get started until late.'

'It'll be months before we can get a person inside,' said Ryan, gazing at the wall. 'We don't have that long.'

'The brick is almost out,' Harlan argued. 'I just need some more time. A day or two.'

Elsa sighed. 'Forget about the wall, we still need a screwdriver. Does anyone have any ideas?'

'Julian said he would think about it . . .'

Ryan shook his head. 'You're going to be waiting a long time. Now if only we had some way of getting him out of his cell . . .'

'*Guard coming*,' Elsa hissed, leaping away from the bars.

Ryan hid the makeshift map pieces beneath Harlan's bed, while Jes emptied a pack of tattered playing cards on to the floor.

They waited for the guard to pass, and when his footsteps disappeared Elsa leant in towards the group. 'We don't really have a clue, do we?' she whispered, throwing down her cards. 'All we've got are a handful of possibilities . . .'

Harlan nodded in agreement. 'You know what they say about best-laid plans. There are too many variables.'

'*Variables*,' Elsa repeated. Her eyes moved around the cell, as though searching for some physical trace of the word.

'Are you all right, Elsa?'

'That word; it rings a bell somewhere. Like there was something I'm supposed to remember. Something about *us*.'

'You're scaring me.' Ryan grinned, trying to make light of the situation.

'Well, I won't for much longer,' she said, noticing a few inmates on the other side were leaving their cells. 'I've got to go. Adler's not letting me out of his sight at the moment.'

Elsa quietly left the cell.

'I'll go and see if she's all right,' Harlan said, and followed after her.

Jes turned to Ryan. 'I'm worried about her. I think she's close . . .'

'To what?'

'Giving up. They said we all would, sooner or later.' She went to tidy away the cards, and her hand brushed against Ryan's, who'd had the same idea. 'Sorry.'

He smiled. 'It's fine. I'm glad I can count on you, Jes. I'm glad we're on the same team.'

He leant across, and for a moment Jes thought he was going to kiss her, but instead he gathered up the paper towels and slipped them inside his uniform.

'A bomb was found in Ludgate Hill this afternoon,' said the female reporter, brushing a strand of hair from her eyes. 'It was discovered by a shop owner who noticed the suspicious-looking parcel beside a dustbin and alerted the police. The Metropolitan Police later confirmed that the parcel contained a remotely triggered explosive device. Fortunately, the bomb is believed to have malfunctioned before it could detonate.'

She paused, then turned to the producer with a hint of defiance. 'Was that any better?'

'Better,' he agreed. 'We'll shoot the interview with the bomb expert and that'll be a wrap. Anyone see where he went?'

'Having a coffee last I saw,' said one of the crew, nodding towards a cafe on the other side of the road.

'In that case ...' the reporter murmured, and slipped a cigarette between her lips, sparking a lighter with her other hand.

She returned the lighter to her coat pocket and leant against a lamp post with her arm beneath her elbow, scrutinizing the small crowd while she smoked.

'Excuse me.'

She turned to see a man in a crumpled suit standing beside her.

'My name is Devinder Jahari,' he said. The reporter furrowed her brow and blew a stream of smoke out of the corner of her mouth.

'My son, Harlan ... he –' the man paused to gather himself – 'he went missing earlier this year.'

The reporter respectfully lowered her cigarette and stubbed it against the lamp post.

'Nothing has been done,' Devinder said. 'My wife and I – we are at our wits' end.'

Shaken by the fraught look in his eyes, she stepped away from the rest of the crew and gestured for Devinder to follow her to a quieter area.

'I'm sorry, Mr Jahari. How old was your son?'

'He would be seventeen now. It was just days before his birthday. He would never have run away, you must understand. He was not a bad child, he was not into drugs, or anything like that . . .'

'I understand.'

Devinder lowered his eyes to the pavement. 'He had been having some *problems* recently.'

'What kind of problems?'

'We took him to see a psychiatrist. They said he was anxious. Paranoid. He was seeing patterns in things.'

'Was he depressed?'

'No.' He shook his head emphatically. 'We made sure he had a good life.'

'I'm sure you did, but it doesn't always –'

'He *wasn't* depressed,' he repeated. 'You have to believe me. He would never harm himself. But he was vulnerable. It is everyone else that I worry about. Do you see?'

'I see.'

'And the police, the newspapers . . . there is nothing out there about him. Nothing! Is there anything you can do? Perhaps a report – there has to be someone who knows . . .'

The reporter noticed her producer waving his arm frantically at her, pointing to his watch.

'I wish there was something I could do,' she said,

stepping away. 'But there are lots of teenagers who are reported missing every week, every month. *Too many*. I'm sorry.'

'Please,' he begged. 'You have to –'

She shook her head gently and offered another mouthed *I'm sorry* and hurried back to the rest of the crew.

Julian waited until it was the middle of the night.

He arranged his pillows under his sheet to resemble a sleeping body and rolled underneath the bed. He carefully removed the brick and reached inside. His hand glided across the ball and the book, and his fingers soon found the screwdriver.

Just what are they planning to do with this?

An attack on one of the guards? No, he didn't think a screwdriver to the neck would be anyone's style. They were going to use it for unscrewing something . . . but what?

It didn't matter for now. What mattered was that he had something they needed. He put the screwdriver inside the torn hem round the ankle of his uniform. He wouldn't have to worry about being searched; he had worked hard for the guards' trust.

Julian lowered himself down again and reached far back into the wall, where he had stored the ibis. He brought it out, wiping his fingerprints off the smooth black sheen.

He twirled the baton-like weapon in his hands, overwhelmed with giddy exhilaration. His finger inadvertently knocked against the trigger and the device fired, echoing throughout the silent hall.

'What was that?' he heard one of the guards on sentry duty say.

Julian shoved the ibis back inside the wall, then pushed the brick into place. The guard's footsteps stamped up the metal staircase.

He rolled out from under the bed, wiped the dust off his uniform and dived beneath his sheet just as the man appeared.

Torchlight swept over him. 'What the hell are you doing in there, Sleave?'

'*Huh?*' Julian mumbled, feigning sleepiness. 'What's going on?'

The torchlight examined the blue-tinted shadows, then scanned beneath the bed and the far wall of the cell.

'It's late. Go to sleep,' the guard muttered, and marched back along the walkway.

Oh I will, Julian thought, grinning to himself under the blankets.

30

'Get up,' said the man who'd called himself Henry. 'You need to be on your way.'

'On my way where?' Alyn asked, climbing to his knees, which still hadn't quite recovered from his fall. He squinted, watching Rayner and the other guard walk away through the snow-covered trees.

'Away from here.' Henry leant down and pulled Alyn to his feet. He was stronger than he looked. 'They'll be back, especially when they realize I was lying.' He peeled off his heavy overcoat and pushed it towards Alyn. 'There's a flask of water in the pocket.'

Alyn looked at him warily. 'Who are you? Why did you save me?' But despite his suspicions Alyn took the coat and pulled it on, feeling instantly grateful for another layer of warmth.

'I don't have time to explain but you need to trust me. Now *go*.'

'Back there, through the woods,' Alyn started. 'There are more of us. We're all being held prisoner. You –'

'I know,' said Henry. 'I know all about it. I don't have time to explain. You just need to get out of here while you still can.'

Alyn nodded, too shocked to completely acknowledge what the man was saying. He started slowly at first, then increased his pace to a run, batting away branches.

His throat burned and ached, and his breath was spewing in a steady fog from his lips. His legs buckled beneath him and he fell, landing on his side. His cheeks felt swollen and stung as he brushed away the ice, wheezing and gasping. He looked over his shoulder.

If that man – whoever he was – hadn't shoved him to the ground and stepped out, they would've spotted him. *It doesn't matter about that just now*, he told himself. 'You have to get up. You have to keep moving or you'll freeze to death.'

Somehow, Alyn found the strength to climb to his feet again. An icy wind strummed the trees and he shivered, wrapping his arms round himself. He trudged on through the snow, making slow progress.

Just as he was losing hope that he would ever find a way out of the forest, he spotted something hidden among the trees: a concrete hut.

As he tiptoed round the hut, Alyn noticed a bundle of cables running from the roof underneath the snow.

He sidled up to the wooden door and listened. When he was sure it was empty, Alyn gave it a gentle push and slipped inside.

Warmth, at last, he thought, and felt the tension immediately start to melt from his shoulders.

At first glance the hut appeared to be a kind of communications outpost for the prison. There was a desk with an ashtray, a large machine with a number of dials and buttons, and a tangle of wires. The far wall was lined with cabinets, each one overflowing with folders and files.

Alyn removed one of the folders and thumbed through a batch of stapled files.

```
MILLS, DANIEL.
COLLINS, NICOLE.
HEATHER, JES.
```

'*Jes . . .*' Alyn whispered, feeling his heart skip. At the top of her first page was a small photograph attached with a paperclip. He snatched the photograph from the page and cradled it in both hands before placing it inside his coat pocket. He flipped back another couple of batches.

```
HART, ALYN.
```

The first page contained a number of biographical details: his date of birth, place of birth, parents' names and date tested.

Date tested? What tests? What does any of this mean?

He followed the text down. *Ability rating.* Beside this was a handwritten scrawl that he struggled to decipher. The second page was just as impenetrable, and was filled with streams of what seemed to be completely random numbers. Alyn continued thumbing through the pages, until he reached the final page to which a note written in red ink was attached:

Will need to take extra precautions.

Alyn soon gave up trying to make sense of it all. He tucked the folder inside his coat and, stricken with a wave of overwhelming tiredness, he curled up on the floor beneath the desk, pulling a couple of boxes in front of him to shield himself from view.

Though he was asleep within minutes, his head was swimming with streams of random numbers, tests and notes and graphs, but, most importantly of all, *Jes.*

31

It had been around four in the morning when a noise jolted Harlan awake. The silence in the prison was oppressive. He removed the coin from his pocket and began chiselling away at the cement. After almost an hour a small mound of powder had accumulated beneath the brick, and across his fingers. Harlan set the coin to one side, and clasped the brick with his fingertips.

It's moving, he thought, pulling it from side to side. The brick started to wobble like a loose tooth.

Just a little more ... He pressed his knee against the wall and pulled back. The brick made a scraping sound until it was halfway out of the wall. Harlan changed the position of his hands and pulled again. The brick was finally free.

He wiped his brow on the sleeve of his grey boiler suit and pulled himself closer, but it was too dark to see anything. Harlan shuffled back and manoeuvred his arm inside. Patting around inside the wall, he felt his hand pass over something: a slender metal cylinder.

A pipe? he thought, but then it moved in his hands. He curled his fingers round the object and slowly brought it out.

'An ibis,' he said aloud, unable to believe what he was holding. *What was an ibis doing inside the wall between his and Julian's cell?*

'I need to talk,' Harlan said, battling through the strong wind to Jes and Ryan during their morning break.

'Our meeting's this afternoon,' said Ryan. 'In your cell. Can it wait until then?'

Harlan shook his head. He made sure no one was watching and showed them the ibis hidden inside his coat.

'Is that what I think it is?' said Ryan.

'An ibis!' Jes exclaimed, almost retreating at the sight. 'Where did you get it?'

'That's not important. What matters is that I have it. That *we* have it.'

'The odds just got a little better. Now if only we had that screwdriver . . .' said Jes.

'A screwdriver?' came a voice from behind them. Harlan quickly zipped his coat and turned round to find a smiling Julian sauntering towards them. 'I might be able to help you with that.'

'Get lost,' Ryan said. 'We don't want your help.'

'Fine.' Julian looked at Jes and gave a shrug, before turning away from the group.

'Wait.' Jes hurried over to him. 'Will you really let us use it, Julian?'

'As long as you do something for me in return. I want to know where this tunnel is. That's what you're looking for, isn't it?'

'How do you know about that?'

'I keep my ears open. You aren't as subtle as you think you are.'

Ryan stepped up to Julian. 'I've got a better idea – how about you get lost? And if I ever catch you hanging around us again, I'll –'

'We'll talk,' said a reluctant Jes to Julian, and then glanced across at Ryan. 'It's fine. Leave us alone.'

'You try anything,' Ryan snarled to Julian, 'and I promise you'll regret it.'

Ryan and Harlan walked away from Jes and Julian just as a curtain of snow began to fall across the prison.

'Look,' Jes said. 'If you really think you can worm your way in, Julian ... it's not going to happen. It's too late for that now.'

'I don't care about being part of your little gang, Jes. I care about the location of this tunnel ...'

Jes frowned and pulled her coat tightly round her. 'We don't know where it is. But we're going to find it. There are plans in the office.'

'Plans? How do you know?'

'*I keep my ears open*,' Jes repeated, folding her arms. 'Whose side are you really on, Julian?'

'My own. It's taken you this long to figure that out?'

'You don't exactly make it easy. One minute you're snitching to the guards; the next you're offering to help us . . .'

If the guards are busy trying to catch you, they won't even notice me, Julian thought.

'What can I say?' he offered. 'I'm complex. I don't plan on being here too much longer. I wanted to say goodbye.'

Jes narrowed her eyes, searching for his intentions. 'Why? Why now?'

'Because I'm innocent. Like you, and like everyone else here. Because I don't belong here.'

He tucked his hands inside his pockets and braced himself against a sharp wind. 'If you're going, you need to leave soon,' he said quietly. 'One of the *turned* overheard you talking. Tom. He plans on telling the guards.'

'What, so he can *sabotage* us? You don't know what you're talking about, Julian.'

Julian was undeterred. 'He's already arranged a meeting with Adler this afternoon.'

'How do you know all this?'

'Because I was in the office when the meeting was arranged. There are benefits to keeping your enemies closer than your friends.'

He began to walk away, but Jes called him back. 'Aren't you forgetting something? The screwdriver?'

'What about it?'

'You said you were going to give it to us. In exchange for information about the tunnel.'

'Information you don't yet have. That seems like a bit of a one-sided deal to me. I'm sorry, Jes.'

Jes marched towards him and grabbed his coat. 'You lying, manipulative, scrawny little . . .'

'I take offence to *scrawny*,' Julian said. He watched as Ryan sprinted towards them from by the fence.

Too predictable, he thought, silently enjoying the prospect of Ryan getting a beating from the guards before he left.

'Give me it!' Jes cried and grabbed and scratched at Julian, who was doing his best to fend her off.

Martin Adler, followed by two other guards, emerged from the prison and sped towards them. The whole yard was watching.

An ibis fired a warning into the air, but neither Jes, Julian nor Ryan paid it any attention.

'Get off her, you creep!' Ryan grabbed Julian round the throat. He drew his other fist back and threw a punch.

'*Prisoner Farrell, remove yourself at once!*'

Harlan tried pulling Ryan away, but Ryan landed a second punch. A web of blood trickled from Julian's nose on to his lips.

'Ryan, stop it!' Jes pleaded, trying to separate them. 'Stop punching him, the guards are coming –'

Before Ryan could throw a third punch, an ibis blasted him in the spine. He cried out in pain and toppled forward, grimacing and writhing weakly in the snow.

Jes threw up her hands in surrender, but an ibis hit her in the chest, throwing her on to her back.

'Stand back, Sleave,' said Adler. 'We're taking the pair of them inside.'

Harlan made sure the ibis was secure under his coat and slipped away into the gathered crowd.

The guards stomped towards the fallen pair, and Adler pointed his ibis at the unconscious Ryan and fired again.

32

Julian tucked the screwdriver into his sock and checked both ways before leaving his cell. He followed the corridor, but drew back upon seeing two guards huddled round the corner.

'We've still not heard a thing,' said a voice. 'Susannah is pressuring Adler to send another team out there. The idea of one of these kids being on the loose is her worst nightmare.'

'Where does she think we'll get the men from? We're already understaffed as it is.'

'Try telling her that. I wouldn't fancy being stuck out there with that lunatic Rayner.'

There was the sound of footsteps, and Julian poked his head round the corner. *So it's true*, Julian thought. *Alyn really did escape . . .*

'Sleave? What are you hanging around here for?'

Julian looked behind him to see a suspicious warden watching him from the other end of the corridor.

'No reason,' he said.

'Well, get back to your cell,' grunted the warden.

As he climbed the steps to the upper cells, Julian spotted Jes sitting cross-legged on her mattress. 'Not that it's any consolation, but I was shot once, a few days after they first dragged me here. I tried to steal some keys out of a guard's pocket. A stupid thing to do, I know, but I was desperate. You know what they say about desperate people, don't you? Who am I kidding, you know better than anyone.'

Julian shifted his weight and leant a thin forearm against the iron bars, watching her. 'I've been privy to some information,' he said. 'Information that might interest you.'

'Nothing you have to say would interest me any more,' Jes said under her breath. 'Now get out of my sight.'

'Before I go –' Julian tossed the screwdriver beside her – 'I remembered. Funny that . . .'

Jes stared at it for a couple of moments, then skewered him with her eyes. 'You did that on purpose, didn't you? You wanted Ryan to attack you so they would shoot him.'

'You give me far more credit than I deserve, Jes.' Julian smiled, and slipped away from her cell before she had a chance to say another word.

'You look troubled, Martin,' Susannah said from the doorway of the office, stepping aside to let him in.

Adler nodded and walked in, palming the damp from his coat sleeves. He looked around the small room. The walls were lined with densely packed rows of books and at the far end was a desk stacked high with projection reels and empty canisters.

'I was just doing some *preparation* for next week's lesson,' she said, following the trajectory of his eyes.

'I can come back another time . . .'

Susannah shook her head. 'No. Sit.' She motioned to a worn leather couch behind him.

Adler sat down and leant forward, planting his elbows on his knees. 'So this is where the magic happens . . .'

'Magic? There's no such thing.' Susannah closed the door behind her and glided over to the desk.

'Seems like magic to me.'

'*Any sufficiently advanced technology is indistinguishable from magic.*' She caught his eyes. 'Arthur C. Clarke.'

'Never heard of him.'

Adler watched as Susannah settled herself into her chair. With the grace of a seamstress she lifted a single frame of film, little larger than a stamp, and fastened it to the larger coil. She held the reel to the light, admiring her work.

'You're here because of *him*, aren't you? Hart. I've already told you there's nothing I can –'

'I know,' Adler said. 'But if we can't find him, I was

169

hoping you might . . .' He trailed off. 'That you might put in a good word for me, with the Pledge. I like this job. I don't want to lose it.'

'I should think not.'

'I've sent Claude out there. He's the best man I have – my oldest friend. If the boy's there, Claude will find him.'

Susannah straightened another piece of the reel and held a craft knife between her fingers like a pen. Slowly, she pared away a small section and reached for another frame.

'I'm sure the Pledge will understand,' she eventually offered. 'They aren't what you think. They aren't *evil*. This is all necessary. It's serving a far greater good. You understand, don't you?'

Adler hesitated, looking at the reels. 'Not *all* of it serves a greater good, though. Does it?'

Susannah stopped cutting. Her eyes rose slowly to meet his. 'Things are changing for the better, Martin.'

Adler scratched his nose and shuffled in his seat. 'So they keep telling me.' He went to continue but stopped.

'I know what your next question is going to be,' Susannah said. 'And the answer is no. There are no ways out of this. We're all players – for better or for worse.' She set the knife down on the table without it making a sound. 'Now, is that what you wanted to know?'

Adler promptly got to his feet. 'I'll make sure the boy is found,' he said. 'I'll do whatever it takes.'

He lurched towards the door and pulled it closed behind him. Susannah made a final swift cut into the reel, listening to the thud of his footsteps until they disappeared altogether.

33

Jes took her tray and meandered through the crowded canteen, looking for Elsa. She eventually spotted her sitting by herself at the far end of a table and went to join her.

When she was sure there was nobody watching, Jes removed the screwdriver from her coat pocket and passed it underneath the table.

'This means I have to go in that vent, doesn't it?' Elsa felt knots forming in her stomach.

'You do want to go home, don't you? To see your mum and dad . . . and your brother, Simon.'

'Course I do.' Elsa looked over her shoulder and snatched the screwdriver from Jes.

'We'll cause a distraction,' Jes said. 'It should be long enough for you to unscrew that vent, get in the guards' room and find the plans.'

'What if the room isn't empty?'

'It will be. The only reason they lock it during chores is so that we can't get in there.'

'You really think this will work?'

Jes put her hand on Elsa's shoulder. 'I know you can do it,' she said. 'I have faith in you.'

Elsa smiled at her uncertainly.

Jes stood up and gestured to Harlan, who was waiting for her signal. He joined her side as they deposited their trays in the collection area. She leant in towards him. '*The man by the door*,' she whispered. 'I can smell the smoke on him from here. We do as planned.'

Harlan took a deep breath and went in the direction of the guard. When he was a short distance away, he lunged towards an unsuspecting boy, grabbing the collar of his uniform.

'What are you doing?' the boy cried. 'Let go of me, I haven't done anything!'

'I saw you in my cell,' Harlan growled. 'I saw you looking through my stuff . . . What have you taken?'

'I – I don't know what you're talking about, I'm innocent, I swear.'

'Break it up, you two,' the guard said, trying to prise Harlan away. 'You can't just go around accusing people, Jahari.'

Jes, who was hovering by the stairs, ran over and tried getting between them.

'He started it!' the boy shouted, making an unsuccessful grab at Harlan's uniform.

'Let go of him,' Jes said to Harlan. 'I'm sure it was just a misunderstanding . . .'

She moved to the other side of the distracted guard and slipped her hand inside his pocket. On cue, Harlan released the boy.

The guard removed his ibis and juggled his aim between the pair. 'You ever think about pulling another stunt like that again ...' he snarled. The weapon quivered in his hands.

'She's right. It was my mistake,' Harlan said, backing away with his hands raised. 'I'm sorry ...'

Jes sidestepped the scene, cutting through the gathered crowd, and bumped into Ryan, who cupped his hand over hers. She gave him the lighter, which he swiftly hid inside his pocket, and he slipped innocently through the onlookers with his mop and bucket.

Ryan left the mop by the wall and went to the toilets. He stood beneath the smoke alarm, snatched a paper towel out of the dispenser and removed the lighter from his pocket. He pressed the button, but nothing except a couple of measly sparks appeared.

'You've got to be kidding me,' he muttered, and tried again. He gave the lighter a shake. This time a small flame took form. Ryan shoved one end of the paper towel towards it and watched as it caught fire, sinking and curling under the spreading flame. He set the towel down by the sink, and removed the cigarette end he had found in the yard from his pocket.

He held the cigarette end against the flame. When

it began to smoulder he placed it beside the burning paper towel. If anyone found this, he was sure the cigarette 'accident' would be blamed on a careless guard. After fanning the smoke towards the alarm a final time, he checked the corridor was clear and went back outside.

As soon as the guards began talking among themselves, Elsa sneaked away and sped down the corridor to the store cupboard.

Inside, she shoved a box out of the way and crawled to the vent. Being back in the cupboard brought back the nagging feeling she'd had since being struck in the head by the ibis. *Something happened here. Something important. Why can't I remember what it was?*

Elsa removed the screwdriver from her pocket and unwound the four screws on the grate as quickly as possible. After a short while the grate loosened and she was able to remove it from the wall. Without giving herself a chance to reconsider, Elsa lowered herself on to her belly and struggled into the vent. Her sweating palms stuck to the surface as she pulled herself in. There was no space to turn round and secure the grate back into place, but it was too late to worry about that.

She could feel her heartbeat against the metal, which sent a pulse through her whole body. She brushed away a frizzy coil of hair from her eyes and pushed on, dragging and clawing her way along.

After several metres the ventilation system divided in two. Elsa paused and tried to visualize the layout of the prison. *Right. It had to be right.* She pulled herself round the corner to the guards' room. *Now to get in and find those plans.*

Elsa started unscrewing the grate, twisting the back of the screws, which hurt her fingertips. She'd pushed out all but one of the screws when the door opened and Adler and Tom appeared, a young guard following them. Elsa fumbled with the grate, almost dropping it.

'Sit down,' Adler said, and watched Tom shuffle slowly towards the chair. Tom was young, maybe only a year or so older than Elsa. His face was pale and his hair curled above his ears. The guard positioned himself behind the boy, not taking his eyes from the nervous inmate.

Adler leant against the wall with a sigh and folded his arms. 'This'd better be good.'

'It will be. I – I have some information for you.'

'About Hart?'

'No, about some of the other inmates. Ryan Farrell, Elsa Winchester, Harlan Jahari . . .'

'And?'

'And Jes Heather.' Tom lowered his eyes. He took a

deep breath and nervously added, 'They're – they're planning to escape.'

'How do you know?' asked the guard.

Tom looked over at Adler, as though awaiting permission to speak.

'Answer the question.'

'I heard them talking about it. They didn't know I was listening.'

Elsa, who was watching the scene from the air vent, cursed under her breath. Adler straightened and turned his head.

She held her breath for so long that it felt as though her lungs were about to explode. Eventually, to Elsa's relief, Adler turned back to the boy.

'When are they planning on doing this?'

'I – I don't know.' Tom lowered his eyes again. 'All I know is it's soon.'

'*Soon* isn't good enough. You need to be more specific –'

'Within the next couple of days, I think. I don't know any more than that.'

Adler and the guard shared a look.

'Will I get anything for this?' Tom said.

'And there was me thinking you wanted to help out of the goodness of your heart.' Adler took a step towards him. 'You'll get privileges when you can be trusted. Until then, you're no different from the rest of them. Go on – get out of my sight.'

'Yes, sir.' Tom sprang to his feet and scurried out of the room.

The guard waited until the door had slammed closed before speaking. 'What should we do, boss?'

'We'll keep them under surveillance for the next couple of days –' Adler paused – 'see if what he says turns out to be true. For all we know he's a part of this too. Diverting the attention while another group escape. We could be playing right into their hands.'

'You really think they'd have such a plan? I mean, they're only kids –'

'They're criminals,' Adler corrected. 'They're dangerous, devious and manipulative. And they'd do anything to be free.'

He was about to sit down, when the fire alarm wailed loudly from the corridor. 'What in God's name ...' He pointed to the wall. 'Get that fire extinguisher.'

The guard grabbed the fire extinguisher from the wall and sprinted out with Adler close behind, the door automatically locking behind them.

Now's my chance, thought Elsa, finally breathing deeply. She finished unwinding the last screw, pulled the grate to one side and clambered out.

Ryan moved out of the way of a charging warden just in time. He watched them with some delight as they hurried along the corridors, extinguishers in hand, searching for their fire.

Reaching the guards' room, he tapped the door lightly with his knuckles and whispered, '*Elsa? Are you in there?*'

Elsa was just getting to her feet. Trying to keep her fingers from fumbling, she quickly screwed the grate back into place. Then she ran to the cabinet under the window and flung open the doors, tearing through folders, notes and sheets of paper. At the back was a rolled sheet. She pulled it out and knelt on it to stop it from coiling back on her.

'*Elsa!*' Ryan whispered again, louder this time. 'We don't have much time. You need to hurry.'

Elsa drew her finger round the shapes, trying to place each of the rooms. There appeared to be a narrow corridor extending from one to the side of the prison, a short way from the east corner by the exercise yard.

It dawned on Elsa what she was looking at. *It had to be the tunnel.*

She could hear Ryan on the other side of the door. 'Elsa, they're coming . . .'

Elsa released the coiled plans and shoved them inside her uniform. She shut the cabinet, then escaped through the door just as a group of wardens emerged from round the corner. The door clicked on its lock behind her.

'What are you two doing here?' Adler said as he approached, eyeing them suspiciously.

Elsa looked at Ryan, then back at Adler. 'The fire. We heard the alarm. We weren't sure if it . . .'

'It wasn't. Now get back to your cells.'

Jes and Harlan strode quickly through the crowd of inmates towards Ryan and Elsa as they appeared in the hall.

'Any luck?' Jes asked quietly.

Elsa reached inside her uniform, made sure nobody was watching and handed the blueprints to Jes. 'The good news is that there *is* a tunnel leading out from the prison –' Elsa turned to Harlan – 'but the bad news is that we can't get to it from the wall by your cell. We can only get there from the classroom.'

'We'll never get in there without being watched,' said Harlan. 'The only times we're allowed in there are with the guards. And the teacher.'

'We're going to need a miracle,' Jes said, raking both hands through her hair.

A miracle, Elsa repeated silently. Why did that strike such a chord? It felt as though she was trying to piece back together a dream, only to find the various fragments trailing like sand through her fingers.

'I have to go,' she said, squeezing past the others.

34

'Prime Minister,' said James Felix. 'I'm glad you could come at such short notice.' He gestured for the Prime Minister to sit and poured two drinks from a crystal decanter.

Once he was seated the Prime Minister covered his eyes and rubbed them with his palms. '*This*,' he said, 'is exactly what I feared might happen.'

Felix took a sip of brandy. 'Let's not get ahead of ourselves. It is just one boy, after all.'

'One boy, Felix. One boy who could put an end to everything.'

'One boy with a rather *incredible* story. Do you really think anybody would believe it? There are times I barely believe it myself . . .'

The Prime Minister knocked back his drink without saying a word.

'He's alone in a forest in one of the harshest winters in recent memory,' Felix said, refilling the Prime Minister's glass. 'I'd be surprised if they found him alive.'

'So the Pledge is quite happy to have blood on its hands?'

'In case you have forgotten, our hands are holding the fate of the country. It's inevitable that some blood will be spilled.'

'I'll take that as a yes.' The Prime Minister took another large mouthful of brandy.

Felix smiled. 'The last time we spoke I recall you saying how fortunate it was that certain incidents had been avoided. I would hate to think of you changing your mind so soon.'

The Prime Minister pinched the bridge of his nose and wearily leant back in the chair. 'Where is the rest of the Pledge? Antonia, Blythe ... even that little maniac Stephen ... I want to talk to them ...'

'They aren't here.'

'Then get them here.'

'Get them here? You really think we have nothing better to do than sit around in darkened rooms, stroking our chins?'

'To be honest, I don't know what you do, Felix. But whatever it is I want an end to it. I want the project stopped. Immediately. I want those children returned home to their families. I want – I want an apology.'

No sooner had the words left the Prime Minister's lips than a tall, broad-shouldered figure appeared behind him. He wore a dark grey suit and a three-quarter length black overcoat. His dark hair was combed into a neat side parting.

'And who might you be?'

'This is Emmanuel,' Felix said. 'My adviser.'

'An adviser? In that case, I would appreciate it if you could advise your colleague to cease the project. At once.'

'I can't do that,' Emmanuel said icily.

'You *can't*, or you won't? Have you forgotten who I am?'

'Who you are is irrelevant. This is out of your control.'

'Just who do you think you are? Felix, I want him removed –'

'I'm sorry,' Felix said. 'If it weren't for Emmanuel, a lot of this wouldn't be possible.'

'So I have you to blame, do I?' the Prime Minister said to Emmanuel, before turning to Felix. 'You're a coward. You're scared of him.'

Felix didn't feel it necessary to grant an answer. The only one of them to be not intimidated was the boy, Stephen. And Stephen was a psychopath.

'It's too late to cease,' Emmanuel said simply. 'The project goes ahead as planned.'

'Then I want no further part in any of this,' the Prime Minister said. 'Good day to you, gentlemen.'

35

Having decided to skip recess, Julian slipped under the bed to retrieve the hidden ibis. As he was crawling on his stomach towards the wall, he paused.

It had been six months ago, and he was back at home. He had not long been asleep when something had caused him to stir.

There was a noise from the garden – what sounded like a clatter. Peeling apart the curtains to investigate, Julian spotted three men huddled round the front door.

His face pressed up against the cold glass, Julian watched as one of the men produced a sliver of wire from his pocket. The man checked over his shoulder to make sure nobody was watching, then threaded the wire into the lock.

Julian snatched his phone from the bedside table. He jabbed in the number for the emergency services and crouched beneath the window, waiting for the call to connect.

There was no signal. *Something was wrong.*

He sprinted to the landing just as there was a soft snap and the front door swept open. Barely knowing which way to turn, Julian darted back into his room and slid beneath the bed.

The men were downstairs. Julian could hear the click of their heels on the linoleum and their raspy whispers to one another.

It's Aunt Alexandra, thought Julian. *This is her fault. It must be something she's got herself tangled up in. It has to be . . .*

Julian had been raised by his aunt, ever since his parents had passed away in a car accident a decade ago. It would not be the first time she had got herself into trouble over money. And probably not the last.

'*Julian?*' called out one of the men. Julian felt a needle of fear in his spine. Why were they calling his name?

He listened as the footsteps plodded up the stairs, with a heavy clump and creak of wood as the weight released on each step. Julian pressed low to the ground. His breathing was erratic and clumsy, warming the nylon carpet.

Soon the footsteps reached the landing. Unable to shut his eyes, Julian watched as his bedroom door opened slowly. He saw two pairs of boots blocking the light from the landing.

Please don't see me, he begged silently. *Just go away, just leave . . .*

But, before Julian could waste another second on prayers, one of the men had lowered himself to his knees, turned his head to the side and whispered, '*Boo*.'

Julian shuddered at the memory. He removed the loosened brick from the wall and reached inside for the ibis. The blood instantly drained from his face.

The ibis was gone.

36

'Someone's snitched on us,' Ryan said, as the group gathered together in Harlan's cell.

'That means Julian was telling the truth,' Jes pointed out.

'Julian? Why would Julian warn us about anything?'

'Who cares about Julian?' said Elsa. 'I'm telling you what I saw.'

'We're not going to get anywhere if we can't even trust each other,' Harlan said. He felt the ibis inside his coat. 'We have to go soon – while we still have an ace up our sleeve . . .'

'Tonight,' Jes said.

'Tonight?' Elsa asked. 'How are we going to do anything with them watching us?'

'Correction – they're going to be watching *me*,' said Ryan. 'They trust me the least out of everyone. There aren't enough of them to watch all of us.'

'It might even work to our benefit,' Harlan considered. 'While the attention's on you –'

'*We* escape,' Jes interrupted. 'We just need some way to get into the classroom.'

She removed the rolled plans from her uniform. The others huddled round her.

'Look,' Elsa said, 'when I was in the vent I noticed it split two ways. One way to the guards' room, the other to the office. You know what they keep in the office?'

'Keys,' said Jes. 'Elsa can get the key to the classroom from there. But we can't distract the guards a second time . . .'

Ryan shook his head. 'It doesn't matter. The guards will come but we let them.' He turned to Elsa. 'I'll meet you back in the store cupboard. You give me the keys, and I can free everyone else. It will cause chaos. Then we all head to the classroom, look for the tunnel and escape . . .'

'Wait a minute,' Harlan cut in. 'How are you going to move around without being noticed?'

'That's where the ibis comes in,' said Ryan. 'Any guards I bump into I'll zap – it'll be the last thing they expect. Then I'll take their guns and give one to Elsa.'

Jes looked uncertain. 'All it takes is one wrong move and the entire plan falls apart . . .'

'I'm with Jes,' Elsa agreed. 'If we lose that ibis, we're *never* getting out of here. And what happens if we get outside? The lookout in the tower will see us . . .'

'So will the guards at the entrance.' Ryan shrugged. 'But by then we'll have enough weapons between us to put up a fight. We follow Alyn's lead: *we run and we shoot.*'

Jes's stomach felt like it was filled with glass. She had been pacing back and forth in her cell, occasionally glancing out of the window, imagining how it might feel to be on the other side of the fence.

'You seem on edge,' Charlotte, her cellmate, said, staring vacantly across the hall.

'I'm fine,' Jes answered, feigning a smile.

She ran through everything in her head, repeating under her breath what she had to do. *Run and shoot,* Ryan had said. *Run and shoot.* It sounded so easy when you put it like that. Too easy.

She was glad she wasn't in Ryan's shoes. Everything rested on him getting to Elsa and making sure she returned safely with the keys.

He'll have the ibis after all, Jes thought, *and the element of surprise,* and she felt quietly reassured.

She tried to put on a more confident appearance as the cells were opened for afternoon recess. Wandering around the yard by herself, a few times she caught sight of the others and flashed them a nervous smile. She looked up at the guard tower, squinting as the snow steadily fell.

Once they were in the woods, they'd be safe. They could all split up. As long as one of them made it out the others had agreed they were prepared to suffer whatever punishment came their way. That's all they needed. Just one to tell the world what had happened to them, and where they were. They couldn't rely on a desperate hope that Alyn was already doing that, however much she wanted it to be true.

As she was considering this, Jes felt cold despair slip between her ribs like a knife; they weren't all going to make it.

Her first thought was Elsa. The girl was only a child, more so than any of them. There would be no way she could keep up with all of them. No way she could outrun grown men. Jes couldn't help but feel responsible for her. After all, it was she who had recruited Elsa in the first place.

Maybe this is why Alyn was always so insistent about working alone, she thought. *No responsibility.*

Jes looked up to find Ryan walking towards her from across the yard. A few curls of his dirty-blond hair peeked out from underneath his hood.

'What are you doing here all by yourself?' he said.

'Just thinking.'

'About?'

'Everything.'

Ryan studied her for a few moments. 'You're not worried, are you?'

'I don't think there's a word for what I'm feeling.'

'Cheer up. We're going home.'

'I'll cheer up once we *are* home. All this waiting around is killing me. It's like the calm before the storm, or something. Why us, Ryan?'

Ryan leant against the fence and folded his arms across his chest.

'I mean, out of everybody in the country . . . why did they take *us*?'

'I thought you were the one with all the theories.'

'I don't believe half of them. I'm just trying to make sense of it all. It's the one thing that gives me some kind of . . .'

'Control?'

'Purpose.' She let her fingers trickle musically across the wire.

'My mum always said I was special,' Ryan said. '*Different*. She always said I'd make something of myself.'

'Mine too. Doesn't every mother say that about their children?'

'Sooner or later one of them has to be right.'

'Sooner or later.' Jes swept a strand of hair behind her ear. 'How are you so calm anyway?'

'Because it's a game.'

'Some game. I'd like to see who wrote the rules.'

'We write them ourselves,' Ryan said. 'I guess that's the scary part.'

Jes tried to smile, but the sight of a group of guards huddled by the gate made her stomach sink.

Ryan took a step towards her and linked his fingers round the fence wire. He looked over at the trees.

'No matter what happens, Jes, it's been nice knowing you.'

Before she could answer, he brushed a finger across her nose, wiping away a fleck of snow.

'What are you doing . . . ?'

He cradled her face with his hands and brought his lips to hers. A cloud of mist spilled from his mouth as he kissed her, and for a moment Jes was entirely unable to respond until she realized that it wasn't Alyn kissing her. She gasped and pulled away, pushing Ryan's hands from her face.

'Prisoners Heather and Farrell,' yelled one of the guards. 'Step away from the fence immediately!'

This was enough to throw Ryan, and Jes ducked past him. 'What was that?' Jes wiped her mouth with her arm.

'Jes, I'm sorry, I –'

'How dare you!'

'I just – I don't know what came over me . . .'

'Get away from me.' Jes stormed back across the yard.

A bemused Elsa and Harlan were watching from the bench. Jes lowered her eyes to avoid theirs and hurried back inside.

37

Ryan had not long been back in his cell when Martin Adler appeared at the bars, flanked by two stony-eyed colleagues. 'Get your stuff together, Farrell. You're going.'

Ryan sat up. 'My stuff? What for?'

'Because the four of us are going to have a sleepover. What do you think?'

'You're being moved,' said one of the guards. 'To solitary.'

'To solitary?'

'So he *can* listen.' Adler laughed and looked at his colleagues.

'I don't feel well,' Ryan said, touching his stomach. 'Just let me stay a few more hours . . . I'll go tomorrow.' It was a desperate ploy, but one that wasn't all that far from the truth.

Adler ignored him. 'You've got five minutes. Anything that isn't packed isn't going.'

'Wait,' Ryan said, the panic starting to mount.

'Please, you can't make me go down there. Just give me another day . . .'

The louder he protested, the more oblivious the guards became to his pleas. The rest of the inmates, however, heard everything. Jes was first to respond, by trying to catch the attention of another pair of guards as they passed her cell. 'Let me talk to them,' she said. 'Just five minutes, let me talk to them.'

'We have enough solitary cells down there, if you want to keep him company?' one of them said, and watched as she backed away.

Ryan is just the first, Jes thought. Before long she, Elsa and Harlan would all be down there. She slammed her palm into the wall.

'They know what's best for us,' said Charlotte. 'They'll make us decent members of society. One way or another.'

'You don't know what you're talking about.' Jes leant her forehead against the wall. 'You're crazy.'

'*I'm* crazy.' The girl smiled and shook her head, but like all of the turned there was a sedated melancholy in her movements, as though she was sleepwalking and not really in the world.

'You just don't see it, do you?' said Jes. 'You've taken the easy way out. You've given up.'

Charlotte sat quietly, unblinking.

'If the rest of you would just *wake up*,' Jes went on, 'we could all get through this together.'

'I have nothing else to say,' Charlotte answered gently.

Harlan watched helplessly as Ryan was marched by the guards out of his cell and over to the staircase. He managed to catch Jes's eye. She raised her palms in a defeated gesture.

It's all up to me, he thought.

He peered out of the cell, making sure there were no guards around, and rolled beneath his bed. Harlan secured his fingers around the brick and removed it from the wall. He set the brick down gently and pulled himself closer, reaching inside the hollow wall.

'Where's it gone?' he said under his breath, feeling for the ibis. *I don't remember it being this far back. I swear I put it here after the meeting.*

Panicking, Harlan began patting around for the ibis. But it was gone.

He replaced the brick, climbed out from beneath the bed and sat on his knees, facing the wall. '*Julian*,' he said.

'All you need to do is crawl along to the office,' Elsa told herself. 'Make sure it's empty, then hop out and take the keys to the classroom.'

She leant back against the wall and closed her eyes. It was a struggle to breathe. 'You meet Ryan in the cupboard. The two of you head back to the cells. You free the others.'

Elsa turned the corridor and began to skip towards the store cupboard, listening for footsteps from ahead.

'Winchester.'

Elsa turned. Adler was marching towards her, his ibis swinging in his hand. He pointed at her. 'You're coming with me,' he said. 'We're going downstairs.'

'Downstairs?'

'To see your new accommodation,' he said and grabbed Elsa by the collar, forcing her down the corridor to where a flight of steps descended steeply into the basement.

'You're putting me in solitary? But I – I haven't done anything wrong,' Elsa spluttered as they reached the bottom. *How am I going to tell the others?*

'That's why you're down here –' he shoved her in front of him and took his radio from his belt – 'because you won't accept what you've done.' He was about to radio for the others to be brought down from their cells but remembered there was no signal this far below ground.

Elsa was defiant. 'What kind of prison won't even let us *believe* we're innocent?'

'A good one,' he answered promptly. 'Belief is a dangerous thing, Winchester.' Adler steered her down a dark, sterile-looking corridor with identical metal doors on each side, the only difference between them being the numbers that had been etched into the steel. Above each was a single, circular light.

'I'll let you pick your cell,' he said, gesturing with his hand. 'You have a lucky number?'

Elsa wanted to cry. 'Please,' she whispered. 'I'll do anything, I'll accept what I did, I –'

'Number ten. That's my lucky number. If you can't decide, I can always put you there –'

'Eight,' Elsa quietly interrupted, her eyes unable to meet his. 'I'll take number eight.'

'A good choice.' Adler grabbed her collar again and shoved her towards the confinement cell. He jabbed a button on the wall, and the door slid open. 'In you go. Quickly now – I have the rest of your friends to bring down as well . . .'

Elsa stared at the empty windowless room.

'I said, get *in*.'

Adler went to push her from behind, but Elsa turned at the last moment, grabbing his sleeve and pulling him with her. He toppled off balance and stumbled just as Elsa darted round him and back through the door.

'You little brat,' he snarled and charged at her. Elsa panicked and struck the button outside the door with her palm. The door closed quickly and Adler began pounding on the steel with his fists.

Elsa looked at the locked door, allowed herself a surprised laugh, then sprinted as fast as she could up the stairs.

38

Julian wasn't sure what had prompted him to look inside the wall that afternoon, but as soon as his fingers found the smooth metal cylinder of the ibis he began laughing hysterically.

Of course, he thought, gazing at the wall that separated his and Harlan's cell. *He must have been digging too.* Julian tried to imagine the look on Harlan's face when he had discovered the ibis, and then when he'd come looking for it again, only to find it gone. The latter was much more satisfying.

'I don't know what's so funny,' mumbled a tired-looking guard who was making his way past his cell.

'This time I'm not letting you out of my sight,' Julian muttered under his breath, and he hid the ibis inside his uniform.

For the rest of the day Julian silently concocted – and dismantled – a variety of opening moves to his escape. He considered calling a spontaneous meeting with the guards with the lure of information; then again, he hadn't seen Adler in some time and the other guards were far less trusting of him to comply. Perhaps he would position the stolen watch by the bars of his cell door as bait, and whichever unlucky warden leant down to examine it would find themselves on the receiving end of an ibis blast. The problem was that if the guard fell at the wrong angle Julian would never be able to reach the cell keys.

Come sundown, his nerves had started to gnaw at him. As the patrolling guards passed his cell, Julian scurried over to the toilet and retched. He was eventually sick and felt a wave of cool relief ease over him.

'Sleave?' said one of the wardens, appearing at the cell bars and peering inside.

'I'm fine,' Julian panted, wiping a film of sweat from his forehead. 'Must have been something I ate.'

The man looked at him suspiciously, then went on his way.

There was a commotion from the end of the row and moments later one of the guards sped along the walkway with his radio in hand. 'Winchester's gone again,' Julian heard him bellow into the receiver. 'She was supposed to be cleaning.'

Elsa, he thought. *What is she up to?*

Then he remembered the guards taking Ryan earlier that day and all became clear. *They're escaping tonight as well.*

*

Elsa had returned to the cupboard and was climbing into the vent when she heard a commotion in the corridor. 'Adler's missing too,' said a guard. 'He's not answering his radio. Get someone to look for him.'

It would be only a matter of time before they found him, Elsa realized. She had to get to the office and find the keys.

She was panting hard and wheezing by the time the grate came into view at the end of the vent. Light-headed, Elsa fumbled with the screws but eventually managed to work the nearest one loose.

Before too long she had removed three. Her hands ached and her fingers were sore. Red calluses had formed on the skin beneath her fingers and her hair was plastered to her forehead. Elsa swept it back across her face, blew upwards a couple of times and set upon the final screw.

Eventually, Elsa eased the grate off with both hands and placed it to one side, then scrambled out into the office.

There was a glass-fronted cabinet of keys on the wall. Elsa tried opening it but it was locked. She sped round the desk and took the fire extinguisher from the wall, raised it above her head and charged at the cabinet. The glass gave way into a concave web. She hoisted the extinguisher above her head again and charged at it once more. This time the glass shattered and fell to the floor in a glittering mound.

Elsa reached inside, careful not to graze her wrist on the jagged glass. There were several sets of keys, with labels beneath them reading STORE CUPBOARD, KITCHEN and CELLS, but none of them were for the classroom.

Julian was in his cell finalizing his plans when a ball of paper rolled to the ground a little way outside.

He sidled over, pulled it towards him and unfolded it.

DO YOU HAVE IT?

Julian thought for a moment. 'I might,' he said loud enough for Harlan to hear. Within moments a second ball of paper appeared.

PUT IT BACK! WE'RE LEAVING. TONIGHT.

Julian tore the paper into strips and threw it into the toilet. He unzipped his grey uniform and removed the ibis. *I guess now's as good a time as any*, he thought, and with that Julian looked around at his cell for the last time.

'Wherever you are, Alyn, I'm sorry,' Jes murmured, gazing through the bars of her cell. 'I wanted you to be proud of me.'

But what was there to be proud of? They were back

to square one. Ryan had been moved to the cells beneath the prison, and Elsa was missing, presumably still in the vent – if she had even made it that far. What more could have gone wrong? At least Harlan still had the ibis . . .

'*Jes!*' A cry from a few cells down. Harlan's voice.

She looked up to see a ball of paper hitting the ground outside her cell and rolling a short distance. She managed to reach it through the bars without being seen, and quickly unravelled it.

JULIAN HAS THE IBIS.

Just when she thought things couldn't get any worse. Jes slumped against the bars.

39

The Prime Minister eventually opened his eyes to see the spitting rain streaking like sparks through the lamp-post light.

'Sir?'

He swivelled round on his chair away from the window to face his secretary, who was standing in the doorway.

'This arrived for you,' she said, and raised a padded envelope.

'Leave it on the table.' He yawned, stretching behind his head. 'I'll deal with it in the morning.'

'You should get some sleep. You don't look all that well.'

The Prime Minister glanced at his tired reflection in the monitor screen. 'Too many late nights,' he said, forcing a smile. 'I'm sure I'll be all right in the morning.'

His secretary left the office with an encouraging smile and her footsteps faded down the corridor. With a sigh the Prime Minister got to his feet.

He ambled past the window, watching the spiral patterns on the puddles, and sidled by the bookcase, letting his fingers glide across the spines. 'Faust,' he muttered with a snort, removing a small wine-coloured volume. 'How appropriate.'

As he was thumbing through the pages, the telephone on his desk rang. 'This'd better be quick,' he answered, nestling the phone between his neck and shoulder.

'I'm speaking on behalf of the Pledge,' said a voice. It was Emmanuel. 'We met yesterday.'

The Prime Minister paused, suddenly alert. 'I know who you're speaking on behalf of. I thought I had made myself perfectly clear.'

'I can only assume this is because of your concerns regarding the escaped subject.'

'The *escaped subject* will bring us all to our knees. I would never have agreed to this had I known the risks . . .'

'Had you not agreed, the project would still have gone ahead.'

'Then why even bother to involve me in this madness in the first place?'

'As a courtesy. Nothing more. An envelope has just been delivered to you. Open it.'

The Prime Minister hesitated, then walked over to the table and picked up the brown envelope. It was heavy. He dug his forefinger under the fold and tore away the seam. Inside were several hundred pages of transcripts from telephone and email conversations.

'These are plans for the riots Felix told me about,' he said, skimming the contents and feeling suddenly alarmed by what he was reading. 'You've been spying?'

'We took some precautions.'

'I – I didn't realize it was such an organized affair . . . There seems to be an entire network –'

'Baying for your blood. Wanting to bring government down. Wanting to start afresh from the ashes. If the project is abandoned now, everything we have achieved will be for nothing. Society will collapse. The country will dissolve into anarchy, and yours will be the first door they come banging on when they want someone to blame.'

The Prime Minister thumbed through another couple of pages, deep in thought.

'We cannot allow chaos to interfere with order, Prime Minister. Do you understand how we deal with chaos?'

'By *clipping the butterfly's wings*,' he answered despairingly, recalling Felix's words on that first night they'd met.

40

Elsa checked that the corridor was clear and left the office. She couldn't face crawling through the vent again. There were voices round the corner. She pressed closely to the wall and waited.

A clammy hand wrapped round her mouth. Tom.

'You're not going anywhere,' he said.

She began kicking her legs furiously and flailing her arms to try to shake him off.

'We're meant to be here,' he went on. 'Why haven't you figured that out? What more will it take to get you to see?'

She ripped his hand from her mouth. '*Get off me*,' she hissed. '*Let go . . .*'

'Guards! I've got one . . . I've got Winchester . . .'

Elsa continued to struggle but Tom held her tight. 'You want to go back to the real world? Well, this *is* the real world. It's more real than anything on the outside . . . *anything*.'

Elsa wriggled desperately. 'You really want to spend the rest of your life in here as a prisoner?'

'There's nothing out there for me,' Tom said. 'You can't go. You have to stay . . . all of you.'

He tipped his head back to yell for the guards once more. As he opened his mouth, Elsa managed to free her knee, which she swiftly brought up between his legs. Tom gave a deflated squeal and sank to the floor, wheezing and red in the face. Elsa cast him a final look, one of pity more than anything else, and sprinted away.

Her triumph was short-lived as she sped down the corridor. Four guards blocked the way, each with an ibis trained on her.

The wail from the next cell made an already-anxious Harlan leap up. He tried peering round the bars into Julian's cell, but was unable to see a thing.

'Sleave? What's going on in there?' said a guard, fumbling with his set of keys. 'Get up.'

The cell door creaked open. Seconds later came the sound of an ibis lacerating the air, and the guard collapsed against the railings.

Julian emerged from the cell, bent down and claimed the second weapon and the keys, and stepped casually over the fallen body. 'I'll be seeing you,' he said to a speechless Harlan.

Julian sauntered past the next few cells to find Jes huddled on the floor of hers. 'Still want out?'

Jes uncoiled herself and rose to her feet. 'Since when have you cared about what I want? All you care about is yourself.'

'We have shared interests,' said Julian and pushed one of the ibises towards her through the bars before he unlocked the cell door. 'More importantly, *you're* going to help me find that tunnel into the yard.'

'If you'd have let us do it *our* way, we'd be halfway through the forest by now.'

'Oh? Last I heard, Ryan was in solitary. And I'd already warned you about that. And without my ibis –'

'*Harlan's* ibis.'

'I'm the one who found the damned thing in the yard under the snow. *My* ibis,' he repeated.

While the turned inmates sat quietly, watching the drama unfold before them, there were others who yelled and cried for freedom.

'There isn't time,' Julian said to Jes, anticipating her next move. 'And how do you know they won't turn on us?'

Jes grabbed the keys from Julian and her coat, then ran to Harlan's cell, freeing him as quickly as she could. She launched the keys towards a cell at the end, but didn't wait around to see whether or not her aim was successful.

Julian hurried across the hall to the corridor and cautiously made his way down, with Jes and Harlan following him. When he reached the end of the corridor, he stopped.

'What is it?' whispered Jes, approaching.

'Elsa,' Julian said quietly. 'She's been caught.'

'How many guards?'

'I can see four. That's four too many.'

'We have to help her, Julian.'

'I'm not risking my freedom for some brat.'

'Without that "brat" you won't have your freedom – Elsa was supposed to get the key to the classroom.'

Julian paused. He looked round the corner again.

'All right,' he said reluctantly, then turned to Harlan, who had been silent up till then. 'You don't have a weapon, so I suggest you head to the classroom and wait for us there. Maybe see if you can find a way in.'

Harlan looked at Jes for approval, and then hurried off.

'On the count of three,' Julian said, raising the ibis in his hands.

Jes nodded and lifted her weapon.

'I'm – I'm not going anywhere,' Elsa said. Her hands were trembling. 'I've just been doing my chores . . .'

One of the guards slowly advanced towards her. 'Think we're stupid, Winchester? We know exactly what you've been doing. Take a look around while you still can. Once you're in solitary, you aren't going to see daylight for a very long time.'

Elsa winced as he pointed his weapon at her. But out of the corner of her eye she saw Julian and Jes emerge from behind the group.

Three blasts were fired in quick succession, each one finding their mark, then a fourth that only clipped the nearest guard's thigh. His leg gave way and he crashed to the ground. 'We need help!' he shouted into his radio. 'We've been ambushed! Sound the alarm –'

Julian sent him still with a final blast. It was easy to see why the guards were so keen to fire. There was something deeply exhilarating – even addictive – about wielding that much power.

'We did it!' Jes jumped over the prone bodies and pulled Elsa, who was picking up the dropped ibis, towards her in a hug. 'Now let's find a way out of here –'

Her celebrations were cut short by the sound of the alarm wailing through the speakers. In the front hall, each of the inmates clasped their hands tight over their ears.

'We're too late,' Julian said. 'They'll lock the doors, the gates –'

'There's always somewhere to go,' said Jes, not willing to accept defeat. 'We have to try . . .'

Julian grabbed her by the shoulders. 'You don't understand, Jes. We're trapped. We may as well give up now.' He lowered his ibis.

'Jes,' Elsa said, with tears in her eyes. 'I hate to say it but I think he's right. I couldn't find the classroom key. It was already gone.'

Out of the window Jes watched as two trucks filled with guards sped past. 'I'm not giving up.' She bit down on her lip. 'I'm going to free Ryan. *I'm not giving up.*'

She started towards the stairs down to the solitary confinement cells.

'I'm going with you,' said Elsa.

'What about you, Julian?'

'Nowhere,' he said bitterly, casting his eyes around at the walls. 'I'm going nowhere.'

41

'Locked,' said Harlan. 'Just as I thought.' He gave the classroom door a futile kick before heading to the office. The door was ajar.

This is where Elsa was supposed to get the keys from. He sneaked inside and his eyes fell upon the smashed cabinet on the wall and the heap of broken glass on the floor.

He examined the plastic labels inside the cabinet. *The classroom keys aren't here. She was looking in the wrong place.*

Harlan spotted a tea towel over the back of a chair. Using his forefinger and thumb, he carefully picked up a blade of glass and wrapped the towel round it like a handle. Clutching the glass shard, Harlan caught sight of his reflection in the window. His eyes were heavy with responsibility.

He went back into the corridor and followed it along until he saw a guard standing with his back to him, talking into his radio. At his feet a pile of collapsed bodies were letting out weary groans. It looked like the others had made it here at least, but where were they now?

Harlan hesitated. Then slowly, almost as though he wasn't fully in control of himself, he crept towards the guard. The piece of glass was tight in his hand.

In a swift motion he wrapped the crook of his elbow round the guard's throat and brought the shard in view of his face. 'The classroom keys,' he whispered.

'I – I don't have them.'

'Liar.'

'I swear it,' the guard cried.

'Then radio someone who does. And make it quick.'

The guard panicked, watching the glass glinting in the dim corridor lighting. 'All right. Just . . . just be careful with that.'

Harlan removed the ibis from the guard's belt and tossed the shard to the floor.

The man tapped a button on the radio and brought it to his lips. 'J-Jim,' he stammered, sensing every tremble of the ibis against the base of his skull. 'I – I need you to open the classroom . . .'

'Why do you need me? Martin has the other set of keys . . .'

'*Quickly*,' Harlan hissed.

'Quickly,' the guard repeated. 'Adler's orders . . .'

He removed his finger from the button and tossed the radio on the floor. 'I did what you said . . . now please . . . please just let me go.'

Harlan released the man from his grip, then, as he turned, squeezed the ibis trigger.

It was the sudden hiss and crackle of static that caused Alyn to jolt awake from a dreamless sleep.

How long have I been asleep? He panicked, pushing away the boxes he had pulled beside the desk, and slowly opened his eyes. In the back of his mind was some indistinct memory of finding a half-eaten roll in one of the drawers. *Was it even a memory or just a dream?* A glance at the crumbs on the front of his uniform suggested the former.

'*Are you there?*' came the sound again. '*Johnson? I repeat: are you there?*'

Alyn rolled to his feet and looked around for the source of the noise. He eventually discovered it was coming from a walkie-talkie that had fallen behind the cabinet.

'*Can't seem to get in touch with either of them. There must be a signal problem –*' Alyn turned off the radio and was about to toss it away when something urged him to reconsider; it might come in useful. With that, he shoved the radio inside the pocket of Henry's coat.

His throat painfully dry, Alyn tipped the contents

of the flask into his mouth until he almost choked, coughing and spewing up water. Panting, he wiped his mouth with his sleeve.

Someone will be back soon, he concluded, aware that there were probably men already on his trail.

Unprepared for the bracing winds outside, Alyn's teeth chattered as he made his way along a slick path of snow, using a branch to propel himself along.

It was after nearly an hour of aimless wandering before he decided to rest. His freezing fingers fumbled in his pocket for the picture of Jes, which wavered frantically in the fast wind. He traced a careful fingertip across the photograph, outlining her face.

Alyn staggered on, casting a look over his shoulder every few minutes to make sure he wasn't being followed, and when he turned the trees seemed to whirl round him like a carousel. 'Just another couple of miles. That's all,' he said to himself. 'The forest has to end somewhere. It can't last forever . . .'

But as he stumbled down a steep hill, confronted with yet another impenetrable bulk of snow-covered trees, he found himself filled with a growing sense of despair. *The forest may not last forever*, he thought, shivering. *But neither can I . . .*

'What are we going to do about the key?' Elsa said, jogging after Jes and Julian. 'There's no other way into the classroom . . .'

'I'm working on it,' Julian muttered.

Elsa looked out of the window at the trucks, one of which had swerved in front of the gates, blocking them.

'You might want to hurry up. Time's running out ...'

Julian stopped, and turned to face her. 'If we hadn't wasted our time rescuing *you*, we might be in there by now.'

'Just shut up, Julian,' Jes said, and pushed open the door to the solitary confinement cells.

Julian blocked the door with his forearm. 'If you think I'm going down there to save Farrell, you're mistaken. You're on your own.'

'Actually, *you* are,' Jes said. 'We're a team. I'd love to see how long you last by yourself.'

She and Elsa hurried down the staircase.

Jes could see her breath as she jogged between the maze of cells. The only light was from the bulbs above each door.

'Ryan!' Jes called out. 'We're here.'

They waited in silence for a response, and then the faintest reply came, muffled behind layers of impenetrable steel.

'Which way did it come from?' Jes said, turning back and forth.

They waited, and eventually heard the cry again, louder this time.

'*Ryan!*' Jes called again, turning the corner.

'I'll go back this way,' Elsa said and jogged to their previous position. 'But be careful, Jes. Adler is –'

Before she could finish, there was a sudden mechanical clicking; the lights above the cells flickered and each door opened.

What's going on . . . ? The ibis was cold with sweat in Jes's hands. She walked quickly, shivering with each step.

Jes continued, but became aware of movement up ahead. 'Hello?' she said, wading through the shadows. 'Is someone there?'

She walked closer. A boot creaked and skimmed the concrete.

'Elsa!' Jes cried out, turning round. 'I don't like this, I think –' She fell silent as the shape moved through the shadows; at first an indistinguishable bulk, until the swirling light from an ibis barrel revealed Martin Adler's face in the dark.

By some kink of fortune, Jes instinctively moved out of the way of the oncoming blast. She struggled with her own weapon but he swiped it cleanly out of her hands and struck her on the side of the face with his palm.

The slap knocked Jes to the floor. A dull, damp throb rang through her ear, then a shrill whistle seconds later.

Adler reached down and grabbed Jes by the hair.

'*You stupid little girl,*' he said, grinding his teeth. 'If you had any idea . . . any idea at all –'

'Please,' she begged, trying to unclasp his hands. 'Please, don't –'

'It's your fault,' he told her. 'All of you. If none of you had even been born . . .'

'Jes!' yelled Elsa from afar. 'Is everything all right down there?'

At that moment she collided with Ryan, who was just emerging from his cell. She shrieked, but quickly realized who it was. 'Am I glad to see you!'

'Likewise,' Ryan said. 'Thanks, by the way.'

'What for?'

'For letting me out. How did you manage to –'

'I didn't.' Elsa looked at each of the empty cells, and froze. 'Adler. He must have found a way to free himself that opened all the doors . . .'

'Wait a minute – *Adler* was in the cells?'

'He was.' Her eyes widened and she started to run. 'We need to find Jes before he does!'

Adler pressed the ibis against the back of Jes's neck. 'Say one word, and I promise you'll never say another thing ever again.'

Jes nodded compliantly.

'Jes?' Ryan called. 'Is everything all right? We need to get going . . .'

The clatter of their footsteps broke the quiet of the underground cells. They appeared from round the corner and froze.

'All it takes is for me to press this button four, maybe five times and that'll be it,' hissed Adler. 'She won't survive.'

'Liar,' said Ryan, edging towards them.

'You don't believe me? In that case I guess we'll soon find out, won't we –'

'Stop,' said Elsa, tugging Ryan's uniform.

Adler smirked. 'You have ten seconds to place your weapons on the floor, or I will fire and her blood will be on your hands. Ten.'

Tears were streaming down Jes's cheeks. She opened her mouth but words failed to make it past her lips.

'Nine.'

'Don't listen to him! You have to get away, you have to escape!' Jes croaked.

'Eight.'

'We're not leaving you, Jes,' said Ryan, and he looked anxiously at Elsa.

'Seven.'

'I'm sorry, Jes,' said Elsa. The ibis was loose in her hand and tilted towards the floor.

'Six.'

Ryan looked at Elsa, and then at Jes. 'I'm sorry too.'

'Five.'

Elsa turned to Ryan. He nodded acceptingly. She closed her eyes and walked forward a couple of steps.

'Four ... three ... two ... *one*.'

Opening her eyes, Elsa released the ibis and returned to Ryan.

'Now get on the floor, the pair of you.'

Ryan and Elsa obeyed.

Adler grabbed Jes's hair, then pointed the ibis at Ryan.

He placed his finger over the trigger.

The ibis *whomped*, but the blast didn't come from Adler. He collapsed quickly, releasing Jes from his grip.

Elsa stumbled to her feet and rushed over, throwing her arms round a disorientated Jes. Jes looked over her shoulder to see Julian standing several feet away with his weapon raised.

'What made you change your mind?' she said, switching her attention between him and the fallen warden.

'Something you said about us needing to stick together,' he muttered. 'For now anyway.'

Ryan offered Julian an acknowledging nod, then lowered his eyes and followed Elsa, who was already moving past the group back to the stairs.

When Julian turned back to Jes she was standing over Adler, with the ibis gripped tightly in both hands. 'I want some answers,' Jes said through gritted teeth. '*Why are we here?*'

Adler muttered drowsily. His eyes rolled back in his head.

'I asked you a question,' Jes said. The ibis was trembling in her hands. 'I want to know why we're here . . . I want to know *who* put us here . . . I want to know *where* we are . . .'

Adler chuckled, and the pain made him wince.

'I'll shoot you again, I promise. And then I'll shoot you after that, and I'll keep shooting until –'

'Go to hell,' he whispered. 'All of you . . . you can all go to hell.'

Before Julian could stop her, Jes squeezed the trigger. Then she squeezed it again and again until Adler's body was twitching uncontrollably on the floor.

'Jes, get away –' Julian tried to swat the weapon from her hands but it was too late; she had already released the shot that had brought Adler still.

A trickle of blood seeped slowly out of Adler's nose and followed the contours of his cheek before spilling on the concrete floor.

'He's not moving,' Julian whispered. 'Jes, what have you done?'

Jes wanted to cry but in her shock she couldn't find

the tears. She covered her face with her hands and turned away from Julian. 'You can't tell them,' she said barely above a whisper. 'Please, Julian, you can't tell them what I did. You can't tell them. I didn't mean to –'

Julian studied her for a few moments but said nothing. Then he turned away and ran to join the others.

42

Harlan waited out of sight with his back pressed against the wall until the guard with the keys appeared.

'A trap,' he sneered, upon seeing his fallen colleagues in a heap. 'I didn't think you had it in you.'

Harlan stepped into view, looking at him down the ibis. The guard started to reach for his own weapon, but finally conceded.

'You're not going anywhere until you give me the keys,' Harlan said, stepping towards him.

'You don't scare me. You wouldn't use that, Jahari. You're a coward.'

Harlan took delight in proving him wrong, then plucked the keys from his belt and ran to the classroom.

Jes, Ryan, Elsa and Julian had left the confinement cells and were hurrying down the ground-floor corridors. They stepped over the bodies of the unconscious guards near the office, as Elsa leant down to pick up a pair of ibises, handing one to Ryan. 'I hope Harlan managed to find a way inside.'

Julian paused, listening to a rumble of approaching footsteps from round the corner.

'There they are!' yelled one of the guards. He fired, the shot only just missing Elsa.

The group charged into view as Harlan was unlocking the classroom doors. He moved out of the way to let them inside.

'They're right behind us,' Ryan panted as they all streamed inside.

Harlan slammed the doors shut and turned the key. 'That won't hold them for long . . .'

'Where's the tunnel?' said Elsa, turning back and forth. 'It could be anywhere.'

She dropped on to her hands and knees, examining the floor.

Julian went over to the large desk at the front of the room. 'I think I know where it might be. Someone give me a hand with this.'

Ryan, who was nearest to Julian, ran to the other side of the desk. The pair shifted it to the side.

'That must be it,' Ryan said, looking at a circular cover on the floor. 'Let's get it off . . .'

At that moment the guards arrived at the doors. The doors rattled and trembled violently, threatening to yield.

'We need to hold them off first,' Harlan said, grabbing the desk. Ryan took the other end and the pair sped with it back across the room and set it in front of the doors.

Julian knelt down, dug his fingers round the cover and hoisted it to the side. The cover slammed on the floor with a resounding clatter, which echoed noisily around the classroom.

The group peered down the hole. A ladder descended some way before being entirely eclipsed by darkness.

'I'm going first,' Julian said. He shuffled towards the hole and swung his legs on to the ladder.

'Open up!' yelled a guard, pounding at the locked doors. 'We know you're in there!'

Elsa looked back over her shoulder uneasily. 'Hurry, Julian . . .'

As soon as Julian was out of sight, Ryan lowered to a crouch and gestured for Elsa to climb inside. She took to the ladder quickly and was soon gone. Jes was next to take hold of the rungs.

The doors rattled and crashed under the force of the horde outside.

'Go on, Harlan,' Ryan said, and looked anxiously at the doors to the classroom. He drummed his fingers on the ladder rungs and peered down into the hole. Harlan was almost out of sight.

The doors roared again. The desk was knocked back some way.

Ryan hopped on to the ladder and climbed down a few rungs. He reached up and pulled the lid across just as the doors crashed open.

'Quickly!' he yelled below and began frantically descending. He put his foot on a rung and slipped. The air rushed up past him, and seconds later he hit the ground.

'Are you all right?' called Elsa from a little way ahead.

'Fine,' he groaned. He got to his feet, a little winded, and hobbled along the tunnel. 'We need to get moving,' said Ryan. 'They're not far behind.'

43

Snow had started to fall once again as the truck rattled back to the prison, returning from a second day's search for Alyn. The smoke from Rayner's cigarette swirled in the slipstream of air from the partially lowered window.

The young guard in the front seat pulled a face.

'Something the matter?' Rayner said, watching him intently in the rear-view mirror.

'N-no, sir. Not at all.'

Rayner inhaled and released a defiant cloud of blue smoke. 'I was sure I would have found him by now.'

The radio in the front of the truck crackled. '*Boss? There's been an incident . . .*'

The driver plucked the radio from the holder and held it over his shoulder. Rayner snatched it and flicked the cigarette out of the window. 'An incident? What kind of incident?'

'*Some of the inmates have broken out of their cells. Farrell, Winchester, Jahari, Heather and Sleave. We –*'

'Sleave? I warned Martin not to trust him. Where is Adler? I want to speak to him.'

'*That's – that's the other thing, sir. It's Martin. We . . . we found him in the basement . . .*'

'You found him. What do you mean, you "found" him?'

'*He'd been shot with an ibis. Several times . . .*'

Rayner felt himself sinking. The surrounding scenery spiralled away, and the snowfall grew dull and distant.

'*He wasn't breathing when we found him. I'm sorry, boss.*'

His heart. Martin Adler had had a pacemaker fitted several years ago. Rayner had visited him in hospital after the operation. They joked that he should take some anger-management classes, lay off the cigarettes and cut down the drinking to one night a week.

'Stop,' Rayner said quietly. The driver obediently pulled over.

Rayner climbed out, walked to the rear of the truck and rummaged under a piece of tarp.

The young guard stared open-mouthed at the rifle. 'Is that . . . what I think it is?'

Rayner said nothing and removed some bullets from a faded cardboard packet, then loaded them into the weapon.

'But Susannah always said if anything happened we had to bring them back in one piece. That's why she gave us these things,' he said, and made a weak gesture to the ibis on his belt.

Rayner snapped the gun shut. 'Susannah isn't here.'

After leaving the hut and trudging for what seemed like hours, Alyn had collapsed into the snow. The uneven ground pressed into his coat and his face was aflame with cold.

Every breath hurt, as though someone was sparking a match against the back of his throat. 'I'm right back where I started,' he said aloud, remembering the last time they had caught him.

He flinched at the half-remembered howl of the ibis, the barking guards as they had stamped across the snow-covered yard to reclaim him and drag him back to his miserable grey cell.

Alyn looked up, half expecting to see the prison fence imprinting its criss-cross shadow on him, but there was nothing.

Nothing?

It took him a moment to understand the significance of this, but quickly it became clear. *He had reached the end of the forest.*

He pulled himself up using a branch and stumbled on, looking back and forth. There was a *whoosh*, and something shot past up ahead. *A car.*

'I made it,' Alyn said.

He almost fell again at the edge of the road. A light

layer of snow was sprinkled evenly over the tarmac like icing sugar, broken only by two parallel tyre streaks.

Alyn jogged along the roadside, looking back over his shoulder, slipping on the slick grass and clumps of snow. When he heard an approaching car, his legs almost buckled. 'Help!' he yelled, spinning round and throwing his arms in a frantic arc overhead.

The car continued to speed towards him.

'Please!' Alyn cried until he was hoarse. 'Please stop, you have to stop . . .'

The car sped by and the cold gust of air blew Alyn's hair back. He limped on with the wind roaring in his ears as though taunting him.

'We're here,' said Elsa, looking up at the ladder.

Ryan glanced over his shoulder and hobbled up to Jes. 'Not still mad about that kiss, are you?'

'No.'

'Look, I'm sorry – I don't know what I was thinking. I was scared. Excited. *Stupid*. You understand, don't you?'

Jes averted her eyes and brushed away a lock of her red hair. 'If this does lead to the yard, we'll be walking straight into their hands,' she said, peering up at the ladder.

As much as it pained the others to admit it, Jes was right. The yard was likely to be swarming with guards.

'There's only one way to find out.' Ryan brushed past her. 'I'll go first.'

He curled his fingers round the cold iron rungs and began to climb. At the top he grabbed the underside of the manhole cover and gently pushed it aside. A gust of cold wet air combed through his curls. He shivered and squinted through the gap. From here, in the fading light, the exercise yard seemed to be empty. He slid the cover to one side and hoisted himself up on to the snow-covered ground.

'All clear!' Ryan called down below.

He scurried alongside the wall until he reached the front corner. A group of guards were stationed by the gates, radios in hand. Ryan pulled away.

'What do you see?'

He almost leapt out of his skin. Harlan was huddled behind him.

'We might be able to sneak up on them,' Ryan whispered, wiping the snow from his already numb face.

Harlan looked up at the guard tower. 'Not with that lookout there. The minute he sees any of us –'

'He calls for back-up. Unless . . .'

'Unless what?'

'Unless we take him out.' Ryan tapped the ibis.

'From here? Impossible. It isn't a long-range weapon.'

'Well, maybe not by itself it isn't,' he added, and

beckoned for Jes to join them. She made sure she was unseen and scurried over with the ibis dangling in her hand.

'We fire together,' he continued. 'One of us has to hit him. It's a given. What do you say? Are you ready?'

Jes nodded. She lifted her ibis, and closed one eye. Ryan also raised his, using his left arm to hold his aim steady.

'Everyone got him?' Ryan whispered. 'Three, two, one . . .'

They each squeezed the triggers. The noise of the blasts combined was far louder than Ryan had anticipated.

While Jes, Harlan and Ryan were occupied with the lookout, Julian dragged a bench from the exercise yard over to the manhole cover.

'What are you doing?' said Elsa.

'Making sure they don't sneak up on us from behind.' He released the bench into the snow. 'What are you hanging around here for?'

'I'm scared.'

'So am I,' he admitted after a moment's pause. 'So is everyone. I'd be worried if you weren't.'

Elsa swallowed hard and watched the others by the wall.

'It seems clearer round this way,' Julian said,

gesturing to the other end of the rear wall. 'Come on. Let's take a look.'

As they hurried along the prison's west side, a small metal door swept open suddenly. Julian tried to halt but slipped on the ice, skidding along for a couple of metres.

The teacher looked up just as Julian crashed into her, followed by Elsa. The trio tumbled to the ground.

Julian regained himself first. '*Say one word . . .*' he snarled, and shoved his ibis into the teacher's ribs.

'I'm not scared of that thing,' she said.

'Then why are you trembling?'

Elsa hopped off Julian's back, who then drew himself away from the teacher, still keeping the weapon pointed at her chest.

'This little plan of yours,' the teacher said, making her way slowly to her feet. 'You do realize it's never going to work? You'll never make it out of the grounds. There are guards at every exit. It's hopeless.'

'Hopeless things have a strange habit of coming true at the moment.'

She watched him intently for several moments. 'Even if you do escape . . . they'll find you. They'll hunt you like animals. All of you.'

'*They?*'

'The people I work for. Don't look so surprised. You must have had some idea.'

Julian pointed the ibis at her. She began to laugh.

'I suppose this is the part where you force me to tell you who put you here. *Why* you're here. The pair of you can threaten me all you want. But I won't tell you a thing.'

'I know,' said Julian. 'That's why I'm not going to ask you. I'm going to ask your boss.'

Julian lifted up the mobile phone he had taken from her coat. The teacher instinctively patted her pocket in disbelief.

'You little thief.' She began moving towards them. 'You give that back or I'll –'

Elsa swung her ibis like a bat. The weapon connected with the side of the teacher's head.

'Nice job,' she said to Julian, nodding at the phone in Julian's hands.

'Ditto,' Julian replied.

44

The lookout at the top of the tower let out a cry and crumpled unconscious against the tower's railings.

Ryan's celebrations were cut short as a truck swerved in front of them and five guards piled out.

'Drop your weapons!' ordered the guard at the front as the men swiftly advanced.

'We're cornered,' Harlan said, backing closer to Ryan and Jes.

Ryan extended his ibis. A sudden blast clipped Jes's elbow, causing her weapon to fly from her hands. *Two against five*, he thought, sprinting for cover behind a plastic bin. He fired, and a lucky shot sent one of the guards skidding over the ice.

Two against four.

Another guard ducked behind the open door of the truck and reached in his pocket for his radio. A shot from Harlan knocked it out of his hands.

'Jes!' Ryan called, scooping a weapon up and tossing it to her.

Jes caught it in both hands and ducked to avoid an oncoming blast.

'Where are Julian and Elsa?' Harlan said, loud enough for Ryan to hear over the barrage of shots.

As if they heard him, the pair emerged from the other side of the building and opened fire.

'I surrender,' the remaining guard said, and dropped to his knees. 'Please don't –'

Elsa blasted him in the chest before he could say another word.

'We leave you alone for two minutes and this happens.' Julian leant against the wall, trying to get his breath back.

Jes gazed at the panorama of unconscious bodies littering the yard.

'How are we going to get over the fence?'

'We were never going to go *over* the fence,' Julian said and stepped over one of the guards. 'We're going *through* it.'

He climbed into the truck, quickly followed by the others. Just as Harlan slammed the door closed, another group of wardens appeared and began firing at them. Julian pulled the vehicle into reverse, losing control momentarily as the wheels struggled to hold the ice.

'You might want to fasten your seatbelts,' he said, peering at the others in the rear-view mirror.

Harlan angled his ibis out of the window and began firing wildly.

When he had built up enough speed, Julian spun the steering wheel round. The truck gathered speed again and crashed into the fence, then skidded and careered from side to side, slamming the group into one another.

A section of the fence slowly toppled and landed with a tremendous clatter. Julian wrestled with the steering wheel to straighten the truck again.

'They're coming after us!' Elsa cried, watching the remaining few guards pile into a second truck.

'Good.'

'*Good?*' Ryan seemed disbelieving.

'That's exactly what I want them to do,' Julian said and glanced at the rear-view mirror again.

Ryan grabbed the seat. 'Unless you've got some plan I don't know about, Julian, I –'

'I always have a plan.'

They were soon battling through the trees. Branches struck and slapped the windshield, leaving the bonnet covered with smears of snow, and fallen pine needles tumbled across the glass.

'I don't think this is a good idea, Julian,' Harlan said, looking back over his shoulder.

'You're welcome to get out and walk.'

This was enough to silence everyone. Julian checked the mirror and drove his foot even further on to the accelerator. The wheels shrieked and the engine roared and clanked.

'You're going too fast.' Harlan tried to wrestle the

steering wheel free from him. 'Julian, you're going to hit something –'

'That's my intention. When I say, we jump.'

'Jump?' Elsa turned to the others in panic. 'Are you out of your mind?'

'No, but you're going to need to be out of this truck if you want to live. Get ready . . .'

Harlan made another grab for the wheel but Julian had already set his sights on a large tree up ahead.

'Get your doors open,' he said.

'Julian, this is –'

'Ready . . . Get ready to jump . . . *Now!*'

Julian was first to throw himself out into the snow, which cushioned his fall. He went rolling for some way, and looked up to see Harlan and Ryan leaping from the truck. Elsa was the next to jump, followed by Jes, who barely managed to escape before the vehicle crashed into a tree.

Julian lay still, winded by the impact. He slowly blinked open his eyes.

Ryan coughed, spitting out a lump of snow. He tasted blood on his tongue. 'Is everyone all right?'

Harlan dragged himself over to a tree to pull himself up. 'I will be in a minute,' he said, inhaling deeply and clutching his arm. He looked around at the others. 'Where's Elsa?'

'Here,' came a feeble cry. Harlan looked up to see a foot poking out of the undergrowth.

Ryan's chest swelled and sank as he breathed out billows of cold air. Gradually he managed to roll on to his side and then to his knees. 'I've hurt my ankle,' he groaned, slipping his hand inside his boot. 'I don't know how far I'll be able to walk on it.'

Julian slowly stood, supporting himself on a branch. 'We need to be past the flames before they arrive,' he said. 'Come on.'

Jes stumbled over to Ryan and helped him to his feet. He leant against her and they staggered forward.

The group were only a short way clear when the truck exploded.

Golden flames wriggled and writhed from the wreckage, gnawing at the smouldering pyre. The air was soon scented with oil and smoke. Each of the group could feel the fire at their backs. 'They'll think we were inside,' Julian wheezed, and bent over, panting and coughing. 'And the fire will melt the snow.'

'And our tracks.' Harlan looked back, coughing violently. His eyes were watering. 'It'll buy us some more time.'

Jes dropped to her knees and coughed so hard that she almost retched. The sinewy smoke was winding towards them. Elsa scurried away, with salty tears streaming down her cheeks.

'We did it,' she exhaled. 'We're free!'

She threw her arms round Ryan, who was caught off balance, and the pair tumbled back into the snow, laughing.

45

The gang trudged and limped along in silence for almost twenty minutes, and when they were sure they were not being followed they huddled underneath the canopy of a fir tree.

'So what's everyone going to do?' Harlan asked, looking at each of the group in turn. 'We should decide on some sort of plan.'

Elsa was first to answer. 'I'm going to find out where we are, then I'm going home.'

Julian looked concerned. 'Home? I'm not sure that's a good idea.'

'You can't stop her from seeing her family,' Ryan said. 'If she wants to go, she –'

'She'll get herself hurt. And probably her family too. Think about it, if whoever is responsible for this made us disappear so easily, there's no reason they wouldn't do the same to them. And our families will be the first place they go looking for us . . .'

'He has a point,' said Harlan. 'I know you're dying

to see your family, Elsa, but you wouldn't want to put them all at risk, would you?'

Elsa begrudgingly conceded.

'I'm going to get to the bottom of it,' said Ryan. 'I need to know who put us there – and *why*.'

Julian removed the stolen phone from his pocket. 'I might be able to help with that.'

'A phone? Where did you get that?' asked Ryan.

'It's the teacher's. But what really matters is that this phone is going to lead us to whoever is responsible.' He turned on the screen, dismayed by the sight of a flashing battery.

'If there's only enough battery for one call, it needs to be the authorities,' Harlan told him. 'The police, the government . . . you need to tell everyone what has happened.'

'We're not calling the authorities either,' Ryan said. 'We don't even know *where* we are, for a start. And whatever this is . . . whoever put us here, I'm sure of one thing – that it's a lot bigger than any of us think. We can't trust anyone.' He turned to Julian. 'Have you found anything on that phone?'

'There's a text message here from someone called Felix asking if there has been any news on Hart. That was sent at six this morning. I'm going to call the number.'

The phone beeped, and the battery light flashed once again.

'You'd better hurry up,' Ryan said. 'That phone's not gonna last another minute . . .'

Julian pushed the call button and turned on the loudspeaker for the rest of the group to hear. They waited in silence while the phone rang. The battery light flashed again.

Come on, Ryan thought. *Pick up the damned thing, whoever you are . . .*

'Susannah?' answered a voice. 'What is it?'

Julian pushed the phone towards Jes. *Pretend*, he mouthed.

'Hello?' Jes improvised, looking unsure. She lowered the phone, covered the mouthpiece and looked at Julian, asking, 'What should I say?'

'Just play along,' he whispered.

'What is going on up there?' came the impatient voice. 'Are you still in Scotland?'

'Scotland,' Ryan muttered, looking around. 'That's where we've been all this time?'

'Shush,' Elsa urged, nudging him in the ribs.

'Yes,' Jes said, doing her best to imitate the teacher's voice. 'I'm – I'm still here. Where are you?'

'You know I'm still in London. I can't do anything until –'

The phone bleeped again and the screen dulled as the power ebbed away.

'You were supposed to be coming down here to

discuss our problem,' Felix continued. 'Is something wrong?'

'Nothing's wrong. Everything's fine. I just . . . I got held up,' Jes said. 'That's all.'

'Susannah? Are you sure everything's all right?' Felix paused, as it all became clear. 'You're not Susannah, are you?'

Jes ended the call, and moments later the screen turned to black. Julian grabbed the phone and dropped it in the snow.

'Felix . . .' Harlan considered, crossing his arms. 'For some reason that name sounds familiar.'

'I guess the next step is to head to London to find him and try to get some answers,' said Ryan. 'It's not like we have anything else to go on, is it?'

'Actually there is,' Elsa said. 'The Pledge.'

'The what?'

'*The Pledge*. I think it might have something to do with the reason we're here.'

'And you know this how?'

She turned to Ryan. 'It was the day after you were brought here. I found something in the interrogation room. A document. The teacher – *Susannah* – must have dropped it in all the confusion when you tried to escape.'

'And?'

Elsa looked away. 'I haven't been able to remember since.'

'That's why the guards zapped you,' said Jes. 'You think it explained why we're here?'

She nodded. 'I think so. And I'm sure the Pledge, whatever that is, has something to do with it.'

Julian looked back towards where they had left the truck. 'As much as I'd like to stand around and share stories, we need to get going. That won't fool them for long.'

The group jogged through the snow, occasionally looking back over their shoulders. Ryan packed some snow into his boot, numbing the pain in his ankle. After descending a steep bank they arrived at a frozen stream, about two metres wide, that wound through the trees.

Elsa approached the edge and tested it with her boot. 'It looks safe.'

'For *you* maybe,' Julian said. 'Only one way to find out.' He gave her a gentle push. Elsa stumbled on to the ice and extended her arms.

'See?' she said.

'I'm not convinced. I'd keep moving if I were you.'

When Elsa finally made it across, Julian leant down and picked up a branch. He shuffled on to the stream, tapping the ground in front.

He leapt on to the bank and fell to his knees.

Harlan stood on the edge of the grass and placed a cautious foot on the ice.

'You can do it, Harlan,' Elsa urged. 'It's not far . . .'

A sound in the distance made everyone look up.

'It's them. They're coming,' Ryan hissed, looking back up the slope with his hand shielding his eyes. 'We need to hurry.'

Harlan turned round and took another step on to the ice. His feet shot from underneath him. Wincing, he clawed slowly forward and reached for the snow-covered bank, finding a handful of undergrowth. He had only just managed to pull himself across when there was a creaking sound, and then the plunging as sheets of ice were sucked into the freezing water.

'We'll find another way,' Ryan said and pulled Jes with him. 'Get going. We'll catch up with you.'

The pair ran downstream. Elsa helped Harlan to his feet and turned to look for Julian – but he had already left without them.

46

When Ryan and Jes eventually found a narrower place to cross, some twenty minutes later, there was no sign of the others anywhere.

In that time it had grown even colder and Ryan began to wonder whether or not they would last until morning.

He held back a branch for Jes and tramped wearily up a steep incline. Large crusts of powder clung to the bottom of his damp trousers. He could barely feel his legs. 'I'm worried about Elsa. How is she going to cope?'

'She's a fighter,' replied Jes, and said no more on the subject.

'When are you going to tell me what happened back there, Jes?'

'I don't know what you mean.'

'In the cells, after you freed me. I know something happened. You've been different.'

'You don't know the first thing about me, Ryan.'

'Has it got something to do with Alyn? Are you worried about him or –'

Jes shook her head.

'Is it about the –'

'Just leave it. *Please*.' The tears were already welling in her eyes.

'I'm not leaving it, Jes. If you don't start talking, I'll –'

'*Just shut up!* It's none of your business, Ryan . . . I don't want to talk about it.'

Her voice cut through the silence. Ryan narrowed his eyes at her and stomped off, shaking his head.

There was a noise from within the trees: a shuffling, the squeak of boots. Ryan stopped and turned. He and Jes shared a look. 'There's someone else here,' he whispered.

'I heard it too. What should we do?'

Ryan turned, glancing at the trees, unable to see anything. 'We run. On the count of three. One, two –'

There was a sudden short, sharp *crack*, which echoed for some moments.

'*What was that?*' he hissed. 'I don't like the sound of it . . .'

Jes gave him a look of mild bewilderment. The colour had drained from her face. '*Ryan?*' she uttered.

He turned, just as Jes was unzipping her coat. Her grey uniform was blotted with a spreading patch of blood.

'Jes, you're bleeding.'

'Ryan, I . . .' She fell to her knees, clutching her side. The blood leaked in streams through her fingers.

'You killed him,' said Rayner, swatting away a branch as he came into view. A coil of smoke swirled from the rifle barrel. 'He was a good man, one of the best. We've known each other since we were kids and you killed him. All of you.'

Ryan thrust his ibis at Rayner and pressed the trigger. Nothing happened.

Rayner held up a plastic fob. 'It's a kill switch,' he said. 'Deactivates every weapon within a fifty-metre radius.' He tapped the rifle with a gloved hand. 'But not *every* weapon, of course.'

He smiled and raised the rifle level with Ryan's chest, squinting down the sight. 'Any last words?' he said, curling his finger gently round the trigger. 'No? Then we can get this over with nice and quick.'

In the quarter of an hour that Alyn had been trudging along the road by himself, three vehicles had passed, each refusing to stop for him.

By the time the fourth car appeared on the road behind him, all Alyn could muster was a disappointed glance over his shoulder before turning back to the seemingly endless road ahead.

'Hello?'

Alyn stopped and spun round. The car was crawling alongside him.

'It's too late for you to be out here by yourself,' said the young Scottish woman who was driving. 'Can I give you a lift into town?'

Alyn tried to speak but found himself suddenly mute. All he could manage was a nod.

'You look like death warmed up.'

'Yeah. I feel it.'

The woman clicked on the indicator and slowed the car to a halt.

'I know you're technically not *supposed* to pick up hitchhikers . . . But I won't tell if you don't.'

'Where am I?'

'Scotland. Could you not tell by my accent?' she said, smiling, but then noticed the serious expression on Alyn's face. 'The cold really has got to you, hasn't it? You know where you are, don't you?'

Alyn slowly looked around.

'So are you going to tell me what you're doing out here by yourself in a place you don't know? You're a wee bit young to be celebrating a stag do or something, aren't you?'

Alyn wished he could tell her everything: about the prison; about the way he and the others had been taken off the streets and from their homes, kidnapped, and forced to repent for crimes they hadn't committed; the guards; and the ibises . . . And that the last time he and Jes had seen each other they had fought, and now he wished with all his heart he could take everything back.

'I – I was camping,' he lied, realizing how ridiculous it would all sound. 'With some friends. I got lost . . . I've been out here for days.'

Only then did a look of concern show on the woman's face. 'In this weather? You could've got yourself killed! Get in the car. I've a blanket in the boot.'

Alyn strained a smile as the woman yanked the handbrake and hurried out of the car. He hopped into the passenger seat. *I'm really going home*, he thought. *I'm going to find out who's responsible* . . . He reached inside his pocket and removed the photograph of Jes. *I'm going to save everyone.*

The silence was broken by a sudden noise coming from the radio in his pocket. Until then, Alyn had forgotten that he had even taken it.

'*The fence is down,*' said one of the guards. '*Get that fire out before it attracts any unwanted attention.*'

A fire, thought Alyn. *What is going on back there?*

'Be with you in a second!' the woman called out from the boot of the car. 'It's a right mess in here. Can't find a bleedin' thing . . .'

Alyn ignored her. He removed the radio from his pocket and raised it to his ear.

'Is there any indication where they might have gone?' said another voice.

'About five metres from the crash site we found some footprints leading off into the forest. They have quite a head start on us.'

'Footprints . . . They've done it,' Alyn said, quickly becoming breathless.

'Get every man to the forest at once,' said another voice. 'They'll be outnumbered. They can't last out there forever.'

Alyn lowered the radio when it crackled again, causing him to jump.

'This is Claude Rayner. I have two of them. Jes Heather and Ryan Farrell.'

At that moment, another sound came through the handset; it was Ryan and he was screaming something.

'You're a murderer!' was the last thing Alyn heard him cry.

Muttering away to herself, the woman lifted out a cardboard box filled with some of her mother's cutlery, then promptly freed the woollen picnic blanket that was trapped beneath.

'At last!' she exclaimed, and rolled it under her arm. 'Sorry about the wait. This'll keep you warm at least until I get you into town. I really should take you to the hospital . . .'

The woman carefully trod across the slippery ice, using the car to steady herself.

'I'm Gwen, by the way. You didn't tell me your name . . .'

But when she reached the passenger seat, she froze. The boy was gone.

Epilogue

Many miles away from the prison, James Felix paused outside the glass skyscraper in central London, which served as a meeting place for the Pledge.

Although the escape wasn't his fault, he knew full well how they would react. There would be shouting, swearing – almost certainly insults – but once the tempers settled down they would sit and talk things through like the men and women they were.

At least that's what he hoped.

It's almost time, he thought, and pulled his sleeve down over his watch, making his way over to the door.

'Felix.'

Felix was startled. 'Emmanuel. You gave me a fright. What are you doing here? I thought you didn't want to be involved –'

'With all the *bureaucracy*? I don't intend to be. What's wrong? You look like you've aged overnight.'

'They know my name,' Felix said. 'And when they find out who I am they're going to want revenge.'

'*Revenge and justice*. I've never thought there was really much of a difference between the two.'

'Is that all you can say? You're supposed to be my adviser –'

'And I'm going to advise you to hold your tongue before you say something you soon regret.'

'Is there another reason for you being here, or have you just come to taunt me?'

'I've come here to offer you my support,' Emmanuel said, and he took a step closer to his alleged leader, who in that moment looked anything but. 'I need to know that you, I and the rest of the Pledge are playing on the same team.'

Felix mustered a nod, which was all that Emmanuel expected.

'Good,' he said. 'Now, let's get this over and done with.'

He stepped inside, his coat rippling as he walked. Felix gave a final, anxious glance at the busy street and hurried in after him.

Acknowledgements

I would like to thank the following people: Claire Wilson, my agent, for her invaluable advice, guidance and support; my editor Shannon Cullen for seeing the potential in my work and her exceptional editorial assistance; Laura Squire for all her input and suggestions; Wendy Shakespeare, Jennie Roman and the rest of the copyediting team; Katy Finch for the wonderful cover; Sarah Topping; Tania Vian-Smith; Nicola Chapman; the publicity and rights teams; Ben Horslen and everyone else at Puffin and Rogers, Coleridge & White; the friends who have shown an interest and given me encouragement over the years – in particular Mike M, Damian and Neil, my future in-laws, Siobhan and Bren; Niamh and Bronagh for their interest and enthusiasm; my mum, Christine, who has believed in me from the start, and never tried changing my mind when I said I wanted to write books as a career. And of course Sarah, my best friend and fiancée, for her endless encouragement and for somehow putting up with me.

THE STORY CONTINUES IN

ANY WHERE

COMING IN 2014

WANT MORE ACTION? MORE ADVENTURE? MORE ADRENALIN?

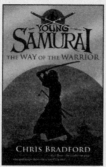

GET INTO PUFFIN'S ADVENTURE BOOKS FOR BOYS